THE 27TH KINGDOM

THE 27TH KINGDOM

A novel

Alice Thomas Ellis

Chivers Press • Thorndike Press
Bath, England   Thorndike, Maine USA

This Large Print edition is published by Chivers Press, England, and by Thorndike Press, USA.

Published in 2000 in the U.K. by arrangement with the author.

Published in 2000 in the U.S. by arrangement with The Peters Fraser & Dunlop Group, Ltd.

U.K. Hardcover   ISBN 0–7540–4152–2 (Chivers Large Print)
U.K. Softcover   ISBN 0–7540–4153–0 (Camden Large Print)
U.S. Softcover   ISBN 0–7862–2628–5 (General Series Edition)

The text of this Large Print edition is unabridged.
Other aspects of the book may vary from the original edition.

Set in 16 pt. New Times Roman.

Printed in Great Britain on acid-free paper.

British Library Cataloguing in Publication Data available

Library of Congress Control Number: 00–090727

For Lillian Cingo
with love

CHAPTER ONE

The story I shall tell begins like this.

Once upon a time, in the year of Our Lord 1954, a woman known as Aunt Irene, who insisted on being pronounced 'Irina' and spelled as I have spelled her, received a letter. It was headed 'The Feast of Blessed Julie Billiart'. Enclosed in its folds was a card with a picture on it of a nice old lady in a wimple, beaming.

Aunt Irene found it irritating. She herself possessed a number of icons, but they represented proper saints, correctly dressed with haloes, long-robed mussel-shell-shaped thighs and angular fingers raised in benediction. Moreover her sister had probably despatched this portrait of a Blessed old girl as a reproach, a reminder; for she feared that Aunt Irene was backsliding, and frequently wrote to say so.

Long ago, in the last century, in the old country, the state had put out an edict that confession should be obligatory in the Slavonic rite, and that any admission of subversive political tendencies should be reported by the priests forthwith to the state officials. Aunt Irene's ancestors, who actually stood to gain by this ploy (for they were great boyars, and revolution would not have been at all in their interests), had nevertheless so resented this high-handedness that they had converted to Roman Catholicism and thereafter been harrassed and hunted until they were forced to leave their ancient estates and flee to the Ukraine. This had given them a taste for travel, and each generation had gone further and further away—to Lithuania and Austria and Turkey and Finland and places like that, or, as the story-tellers would have it, across 27 lands and 30 countries until they came to the 27th kingdom—and at last Aunt Irene had come to rest in Chelsea and her sister in a convent in Wales.

Aunt Irene had no desire to visit the land of her fathers, which was now run by insensitive people in heavy overcoats and homburg hats, but she believed that her genes had somehow become imprinted with intangibles, that even her retina was designed to appreciate vast melancholy spaces and beautiful, strange artefacts; and when she closed her eyes she would sometimes see the fretted wooden balcony of a *dacha* overlooking a grey garden hung with tangled vines. She claimed to be able to smell snow long before it was observed preparing to precipitate on Dogger, Bight and Finisterre; and in her ears sometimes sounded the doomed wails of beribboned brides flung from *troikas* to distract and temporarily assuage the ravening wolf packs roaming the steppes and forests in search of honeymoon couples.

She was slothful and generally cheerful, but when her depression threatened to become depthless she would go not to Holy Redeemer (the church the Catholics had to make do with since the sycophantic followers of Henry VIII had had the *chutzpah* to annexe the church of St Thomas More, who had been murdered by that same king) but to the Orthodox establishment, conveniently situated in Ennismore Gardens. There, at the appropriate moments, she would beat her forehead on the floor, and her dessicated ears would swell with the splashing syllables and deep tones of the chanting priests, and she would emerge refreshed.

She read her letter again, and because it made her cross she ate another piece of toast, reflecting that it was always one's family who annoyed one most and made one fat. Simply that her sister was now called 'Reverend Mother' made Aunt Irene cross and inclined to put too much butter on her toast. As far as she was concerned, her sister was a naughty girl called Berthe, with dark flying hair and a dipping hem to her dress. She hadn't agreed particularly well with that girl, but she had forgotten; and she resented her transformation into the stately virgin in the stiff robes that were so alarmingly clean. Aunt Irene herself was clean, but her clothes were soft and

3

scented.

'Kyril,' she called to her nephew, wishing to know what he would think of his Aunt Berthe's latest idea. 'If you don't come now you'll have no breakfast at all. Read this,' she added, as he appeared in the doorway.

Kyril kicked the cat, who was sitting in front of his chair gazing hopefully up at the table, and sat down.

'Don't be rude to Focus,' said Aunt Irene automatically, passing over the letter.

'I can't be bothered to read it,' said Kyril. 'Tell me what's in it.' He was small and graceful and the working-class neighbours described him as ' 'ahn'some'. His mahogany-coloured hair was parted in the middle like the hair of a Greek or Russian patriarch, and his eyelids were short, falling straight down from his brows like blinds. When he raised them, his eyes were clear blue and pupilless. His upper lip, too, was short, causing him to lisp very slightly. Most women and some men found him irresistible, which had proved bad for his character. Men who didn't find him attractive often wanted to beat him up; but Kyril had had TB, which had saved him from serving in the armed forces but deprived him of a lung, and these men were therefore morally bound to stay their hands. This was just as well for them, in fact, for Kyril had learned at school to be an accomplished and unscrupulous fighter, not above biting bits off his assailants. He had a

4

long scar on his back where his lung had been removed, and like St Thomas More favoured one shoulder, which gave him the seeming of a king's youngest son—beautiful, innocent and unjustly dealt with. In truth his psyche resembled more that of a witch—sardonic and very old.

'Your Aunt Berthe wants me to take in some girl called Valentine from the convent. I can't imagine why. It'll be such a nuisance,' whined Aunt Irene.

'Then don't,' said Kyril, who was a total hedonist.

Aunt Irene, who was only a partial, or flawed, hedonist, was surprised. It hadn't occurred to her to refuse. People who refused were unlikeable, costive and mean. 'How,' she said, not in the spirit of enquiry.

'Just say *no*,' said Kyril.

'I can't,' said Aunt Irene. 'Berthe says she comes from some island miles and miles away. Much too far to go to!'

Kyril shrugged. 'Then take her,' he said.

Aunt Irene thought Kyril remarkable. It was he who had defined her: at his birth she had become an aunt, and his mother's prompt death had ratified and strengthened her position. Her two short marriages had done nothing to change this. It was as her nephew's aunt that she existed, and she was quite content that this should be so. Nevertheless Kyril could be exasperating.

5

'I do wish you'd read it,' she said. 'You might see something I've missed.'

'There's a picture of an old lady in a tent,' said Kyril, picking up the card.

'It's not a tent,' protested Aunt Irene, moved to defence. 'It's her wimple. I want you to read the *letter*, and see if you can tell whether there's something *wrong* with this girl.'

'If it doesn't say so,' said Kyril, 'there's absolutely no way of knowing, because neither of us has second sight.'

'*I* have,' claimed Aunt Irene at once.

'Then you should know,' said Kyril. 'Or perhaps you'd like me to cut up Focus and you can read his entrails?'

Focus was as white as frost. He had long floating fur and eyes the amber of the unclouded peat-stained streams of early spring bearing the late winter's floods—like whisky and water—as though to warm the pale mist of the fur that surrounded his Persian person. He had a flat, rather foolish, face, like a flower, which belied the intelligence and strength of purpose that lay behind it between his symmetrical ears. His appearance was against him, for it is difficult to take seriously something that looks like a down pillow turned inside out. Despite the apparent diminution in size consequent to a cat upon total immersion, Focus looked more formidable when he'd been for a dip. He was unusual in that way. He

6

enjoyed swimming—in the sea.

He and his owner glared at Kyril.

'Don't be horrible,' said Aunt Irene, 'and drink your coffee.'

*　　*　　*

Reverend Mother was frowning. Instead of studying the week's accounts she was sitting at her desk staring at the door. She hadn't wanted to dismiss Valentine, who was a most promising postulant and had come over the seas with radiant recommendations from the nuns who had taught her; but one of those undeniable convictions which seldom trouble the non-religious had arisen in her consciousness as clear as a great fish from the nebulous waters. She had tried to ignore it, but her relationship with God was intimate, domestic; and she had finally conceded, as any woman concerned with keeping the world going must concede, to an autocratic master, since argument would be useless, time-wasting and ultimately detrimental to her dependants. She gazed at a view of the Resurrection placed, cheeringly, to the right of a great crucifix. 'You must go,' she had said to Valentine. 'You have tested your vocation here, and for a while you must test it in the world.'

She opened the drawer of her desk and looked at what it contained, wondering why

7

she hadn't mentioned it to Valentine. It was, after all, the real reason for her decision. Then she wondered why people thought the conventual life so simple and straightforward. The problems of the world were as nothing compared with the problems of the Enclosure.

She was glad she had thought of Irene, since Valentine now had no family. At least, reflected Reverend Mother, she would be safe there; for as far as she was concerned her sister was still the lazy generous girl she had known in their father's house, lying under the lilac, cushioned on the clover.

*　　　*　　　*

Kyril finished his coffee and rose. 'Little Mr Sirocco will have to go,' he said. 'They can hardly share a bedroom.'

'It's time he went anyway,' said Aunt Irene. 'He smokes in bed. He's a fire hazard. You'll have to tell him.'

'All right,' said Kyril, quite pleased with this chance to be legitimately unkind. He was fed up with little Mr Sirocco, who had turned out to be resolutely virtuous and very earnest in a dim and blundering fashion, and had quite refused to produce any free samples from the firm of wine shippers where he worked. 'You must give up taking in deserving cases,' he said. 'They're boring.'

Aunt Irene refrained from pointing out that

most of the people who came to stay in Dancing Master House were people with whom Kyril had got drunk, who had had to spend the night and who then had seen no immediate reason to leave, since Aunt Irene's domestic regime was comfortable beyond the expectations of most of the indigenous population. They had once had a refugee to stay—a middle-European relation—but had hastily got rid of her when one day, as they drove from Middlesex into Kent, she had insisted on stopping the Morris and running backwards and forwards over the boundary, waving her arms—because, she explained, she had never before been able to cross a border without interrogations, passports and papers.

As Aunt Irene said, there were limits. It wasn't kindliness that led her to house and feed people; but nor was it the motive of the witch who had hoped to eat Hansel and Gretel—she wasn't very interested in anyone except Kyril. It was more that she was an artist, that she needed an appreciative audience, and since her skill lay in cooking and housekeeping people weren't merely her audience but in a sense also her raw materials, to be disposed and manipulated as the fancy took her.

'This girl will need feeding up after the convent,' she said. 'Those nuns eat lentils all the time. This will be a nice change for her.'

'It certainly will,' said Kyril.

'I don't know why you say it like that,' said Aunt Irene, who had also realised offendedly that her house wasn't an entirely suitable place for a good girl. 'You talk as though we were a brothel.'

'We are,' said Kyril thoughtfully; 'we are.'

*   *   *

Valentine woke early to the cry of a bird calling on a single note—a mournful desultory cry in the clear unfurnished dawn of early spring, echoing like the cry of someone in intolerable grief alone in an empty house. It went on calling, high on the vaulted morning, until Sister Ann came by with the waking bell.

Valentine joined the silent nuns in chapel.

'Introibo ad altare Dei,' said the priest. *'Ad deum qui laetificat juventutem meam.'*

Breakfast was sad; the bread dry, the salt savourless. The refectory shadows seemed more like the final darkness of night than the boundaries of morning, and the windows were grey with hopelessness. Even the matutinal smells of baking and washing and fruit and guttered candles held not hope but memories and the implication that what had been would continue to be, but just for a while, for experience was finite, and all things but night must end.

Only Valentine liked that morning: the long sweep of sisters dressed in the brown of old

10

leaves, their banded foreheads white as the walls, and the grave fall of scapulars to their sandalled feet. But then it was easier for her, for she wouldn't be tormented by the marriage of memory with things, by the emptiness of chairs and beds and rooms and gardens—and besides, she knew beyond all doubt that she would come back. The sisters would have understood this if she had been permitted to tell them, for they themselves viewed with tranquillity the prospect of their own departures through death, secure in the sure and certain hope of resurrection. It was temporal departures that saddened them, for they were unattended by the comforting glory of ritual and not distinguished by the certainty of return. Valentine said none of this, but smiled as well as she could, for to leave even for a little while was not without pain.

She went through the convent gate, where the winter-flowering jasmine threw a few chill drops of cold rain on her, and the portress at the Turn wept as she left.

Sister Ann drove her to the station in the convent brake and said goodbye.

'Goodbye,' said Valentine, alone on the platform. 'I am Eve, great Adam's wife,' she said, regretting sin, who had never committed it.

The train was hot and unclean. It took her swiftly under the tumbling skies of the border and into the Midlands where the spring sky

11

was beast-grey and the hedgerow blossom, white as death, danced against it. The banks sped by, arrowed like Crecy, until all the trees and the fields were left behind and the train came to London.

*   *   *

Aunt Irene spoke firmly to her cleaning lady. 'Mrs Mason,' she said, 'we must clean out little Mr Sirocco's room and make it ready for a . . .' She paused. How to describe Valentine? A nun? No. 'For a girl,' she concluded.

'A *girl*,' said Mrs Mason, with ironic intent. 'Well, well.' Neither of these ladies was satisfied with the other, each being aware with a different degree of resentment that Mrs Mason was not designed by nature or nurture to be a char.

Mrs Mason was the widow of a major—or rather the wife, for her husband wasn't actually dead. Major Mason spent most of his time in a pub on the Kings Road and the rest of the time either going there or coming back, and nobody had ever seen him sober. He was invariably the first to arrive and the last to leave. At precisely 10.45 a.m. he would rise from the leather armchair in his basement sitting-room and ascend the area steps, his eyes set implacably in the direction of the Bunch of Grapes, and as the barman drew the bolt on the door of the spit and sawdust he would enter, silently. He seldom spoke. Sometimes, very rarely, he would engage in speech with a passing stranger and tell anecdotes which, being at once both scatological and sentimental, were highly repulsive to most people. He would describe how, when he had really overdone it, his wife (who, he averred, devotedly loved him) would undress and wash him as though he were a baby. At this point the unfortunate stranger would understand that the Major was in some sense mad and hasten away.

Mrs Mason had just seen her husband off. With her dustpan and brush she had swept up the mound of greyish, evil-smelling flakes which fell from him and covered the ground wherever he sat. She had polished the regimental cigarette box and straightened the net curtains, which were still redolent of dust and the winter's fog, though she had just washed them. The windows were fast shut with years of paint, and the flat was stuffy, as well as dingy and dark. Outside, bars were set to discourage the casual thieves who sometimes nipped down the area steps to see what they could see.

Mrs Mason looked now through Aunt Irene's rich windows, sparkling like spring water and framing fat pink shrubs that grew with child-like health in the tiny London garden. It was a backyard, really, but as unlike her own, which contained all the dustbins from the flats above, as she herself was unlike Aunt Irene—and yet she lived only a few minutes' walk away and their early circumstances had been surely not dissimilar.

It was *money*, thought Mrs Mason with dull despair, as she put aside her high-heeled pumps and pulled on her comfortable shoes preparatory to hoovering the bedrooms. Money. The war had ruined so many lives while enriching the unworthy and the unscrupulous—the Major had been all right until a small error of judgment had caused a number of his men to be blown to gobbets before his eyes—and even now she deeply distrusted people with money, especially foreigners. The words 'fifth column', 'profiteer', 'black market', 'spiv' still played a large part in her mental vocabulary.

She ran her tongue over her front teeth, which were waxed with lipstick. 'Has Mr Sirocco gone then?' she asked.

'Yes,' said Aunt Irene, rather inaccurately since, although it was true that he wasn't here, he didn't yet know that he wouldn't be allowed to return.

'A girl,' mused Mrs Mason. 'Goodness.'

After a while she leaned over the banisters, hoover flex in hand. 'Your nephew will be sleeping in the same room?' she enquired above the loud susurration.

'The same room as what?' asked Aunt Irene.

14

'The same as the one he's in now,' enunciated Mrs Mason, who hadn't meant that at all.

Aunt Irene was amused at this clumsy demonstration of spite. 'But *of course*,' she said smoothly, gazing upwards, her kitten-eyes wide.

'Ah,' said Mrs Mason, nodding.

CHAPTER TWO

'I am Aunt Irene,' Aunt Irene told the girl who stood before her in the hallway. 'Pronounced "Irene" to rhyme with "serener", rather than "Irene" to rhyme with "insane", or "Irene" to rhyme with "teeny weeny", or "Irene" to rhyme with "unseen".'

'Yes,' said Valentine.

'I expect my sister told you,' said Aunt Irene.

'Yes,' said Valentine.

*   *   *

The nuns seemed low in spirit, and the convent a little dull—bereft, as though the altar flowers had died. Well, thought Reverend Mother, it was no good looking to Valentine to brighten the days. The master of this place was, after all, a jealous God, and Valentine had been vivid and alien—like a tropical angel,

bright-winged in the forest darkness. Reverend
Mother rebuked herself for fancifulness.

*   *   *

'I expect you'd like to wash,' said Aunt Irene
leading the way upstairs. 'The bathroom is
here, and your bedroom is there.'

There were gilt cherubs in the bathroom
holding white towels through rings in their
mouths, and the walls and ceiling were made
of looking-glass. Narcissus could lie in his
nacreous bath and, gazing upward, see all of
himself reflected. Even the door was a
mirror—something that doors should not be.

There were no mirrors in the convent. The
nuns never saw their own faces, except when
the more curious might raise their heads to
catch a glimpse of themselves in the winter-
blackened windows on the way to chapel. But
that was a peccadillo and seldom done. For
evidence that they existed, they relied on the
attention of their sisters and the awareness of
God.

Valentine now saw her face reflected in the
mirror above the wash basin. Surprised, she
turned her eyes away: she had seen only pale
faces for a long time now. She glanced down at
her familiar hands and, reassured, washed
them in scented soap that frothed like the
foam of wine-dark seas. She looked out of
place, she thought, ridiculous, with her

16

cropped hair and black frock in the shimmering shell of a room, from which you would expect, at least, the Cyprian to emerge.

Aunt Irene gazed in the Regency mirror in the hallway when she went downstairs. 'Mirror, mirror on the wall,' she addressed it, her hand to her mouth to hide a slightly shocked smile. She hadn't expected to be faced with someone more beautiful than Kyril. Her own looks had gone—disappeared under waves of creamy, curdling flesh. How odd that bones, reminders of old mortality, should be considered essential to beauty in this perverse age. What of Titian and Rubens? And Michelangelo—no, perhaps not Michelangelo, whose women were really men, cursorily emasculated, with breasts like poached eggs placed randomly on their chests. Then what of those African potentates who force-fed their favourite wives on milk and honey until the beloved women could scarcely move and had to be rolled around. Such extravagant black fatness must have a beauty of its own. Valentine was tall and slim.

'Come down when you're ready,' she called.

Valentine did not speak, since at the moment she had nothing to say. She went into her bedroom. It was warm and full of pretty little things. Primitive paintings in bird's-eye maple frames hung on the walls, their innocence mocked by the deliberation of their surroundings. The walls were papered with a

17

pattern of sweet peas clambering up faintly delineated bamboo poles. Another looking-glass in a Georgian stand on a rosewood table was flanked by a porcelain bowl of *pot-pourri*. The bed frame was of gleaming brass, and on the wide shining floorboards lay a rug worked with formalised Moorish birds and flowers.

On the whole, it made her think of hell.

*   *   *

'She's *black*,' remarked Kyril, who had come home early to see what fate had brought to his attention. He had been looking forward to teasing a plain pious convent girl, all squint and linsey-woolsey; and while he still retained every intention of teasing Valentine he had got off on the wrong foot, his cleverness disoriented by her unexpectedness. She was a composed young woman who seemed already to find him not irresistible.

'I had noticed,' said Aunt Irene. 'I haven't gone blind.' She stopped speaking and rattled the teapot as Valentine came in with the scones.

'Blast,' said Kyril as he spilled a little *lapsang souchong* over his corduroyed knee. 'I hate afternoon tea. Why do you do it?'

'We must observe the decencies,' said Aunt Irene. 'We must remember Beluga, and Fabergé and the 'Ermitage.'

'Oh, for God's sake,' said Kyril, dashing at

18

his damp knee with a frail white hand. 'Sometimes you bewilder me.'

Aunt Irene, who had been partly joking and partly attempting to give Valentine a brief idea of their background, grew annoyed with her nephew.

'*Déclassé* is one thing,' she said sharply, 'but you go too far.'

'Oh darling,' said Kyril, 'I have always been too far. You have only yourself to blame.'

Flattered, Aunt Irene grew mild again.

Valentine took out the cups.

'She obviously means to help,' said Aunt Irene. 'Does she strike you as awfully sad?'

'No,' said Kyril, 'just average.'

'Your aunt says she's had a tragic life. I had somehow assumed she'd been hungry and beaten, but she doesn't look like that.' Aunt Irene went through the various forms of tragedy that afflict the living: madness and death duties for the upper classes, hunger and indignity for the lower, the eldest son's marriage to the girl on the haberdashery counter for the middle. Knowing very little of tropical society, Aunt Irene couldn't imagine in which of these categories Valentine would be, at home on her island. Certainly she seemed to have undergone no physical hardship. Her skin and her eyes and her hair all shone with a copperish lustre, and her slenderness was the slenderness of health not deprivation.

'Someone must have died,' said Aunt Irene. 'That's tragic. I wish I could find Berthe's letter.' She looked in the drawer of the Sheraton desk and then on the mantelpiece, where a number of invitation cards had been shuffled into one deck. 'Mrs Mason's tidied it,' she said. 'I believe she takes the post home to read at leisure. No wonder I can never find those dreary forms.'

'You throw forms away,' Kyril reminded her. 'You put them under the cat's meat, you make spills of them, and sometimes you tear them up into lots of little bits.'

'Nonsense,' said Aunt Irene.

'They'll catch up with you one day,' said Kyril.

*　　　*　　　*

Valentine woke early as ever the next morning—rose, assumed her black frock and went downstairs. Kyril stirred as she did so. The third tread from the bottom creaked. Kyril usually woke when he heard it, in hope or fear that some lover was going or coming, but now the carriage clock beside him revealed that, in his terms, it was the middle of the night, and he slept again.

Valentine stepped over Focus stretched out on the bottom stair and went down to the basement, to the kitchen and dining-room.

The dining-room walls were distempered

20

dull pink, and the tables and chairs were of olive-green *papier mâché*, painted with faded peonies and lotus blossoms and edged in dulling gilt. A seventeenth-century representation of St Sebastian stuck full of arrows like a porcupine hung on the far wall. It seemed to Valentine unsuitable that a Christian martyr should be deployed merely as a decorative object, and anyway the artist was a numbskull, since the person in the picture was clearly about to expire and St Sebastian had, in fact, been flogged to death early in the fourth century. On the table were some warlike scarlet tulips in a Chinese bowl writhing with dragons. It was a room for the night time and looked at once wicked and pitiful in the dawn light, like a dance hall or the remains of a Sabbat on the morning after. The kitchen, however, had the innocent importance of an essential place, despite the evidence of a cynical artistic sensibility—things left over from the eighteenth and nineteenth centuries twinkled self-consciously on the dull wooden shelves, astonishingly existent when their makers and past owners had crumbled into dust. Kitchens, being necessary, were as holy as bread and water, and were at their best, in peaceful readiness, at this innocent time of day. The sins of the night had all been committed by now, the perpetrators in flight, in hiding or exhaustedly asleep, and the sins of the day lay ahead. Only the industrious, the

21

virtuous or the painfully ill were awake at this hour, and at this hour even Aunt Irene's tasteful pots and pans seemed like the vessels of God. The walls were olive green, the woodwork olive brown, the pans a pink-hued copper, and the kitchen china flowered and fragile and old.

The convent refectory was white as bone; the table long and bowed, not with the weight of viands, but with its own. The nuns ate very plain food and every last crumb, for waste was unholy. They cut their bread into three pieces to remind them of the Trinity and they tipped their soup bowls towards themselves, for it would be discourteous to spill soup over the table into the lap of the sister opposite.

Valentine moved like a fish through water, accomplishedly, barely stirring the silence. It was a trick nuns learned: to be very quiet in case of still small voices. She opened the half-glassed door and stepped into the yard. Someone had wrought a work of *trompe l'oeil* on the opposite wall—a long path seemed to lead through rows of oleanders to a distant gate: many a drunkard had further bruised a coarsened nose attempting that impossible path. A mulberry tree in a neighbouring garden dipped its branches down into the morning shadows.

There was a bird here too. It chirruped idly somewhere out of sight. Focus came out to sniff the pink primulas which grew in flower-pots under the wall and approve the morning that promised to develop into a fine day such as cats enjoy. He wound stoutly round Valentine's ankles like a cat trying to knit something. Aunt Irene would have been surprised to see this: Focus was generally considered something of a misanthrope.

Aunt Irene and Kyril both came downstairs at eight o'clock.

'Do you habitually rise before God?' enquired Kyril of Valentine, in the light clear tone that was one of the characteristics that made people want to beat him up. His mouth was set in the semi-permanent archaic smile which was another of those characteristics. The head prefect at his school had maintained that it was that very smile that had caused the Ancient Greeks to become extinct. It was a marvel, he had said, that with that grin on their faces the Greeks had got as far as they had before everyone else murdered them.

Valentine looked at him but did not speak.

'Why did the nuns expel you?' Kyril asked, venturing a little further, his head bent in an attitude so suggestive that Aunt Irene felt that, if he had been a stranger and addressing her, she would have emptied the *orange pekoe* over him. Sometimes she was so afraid for him with his reckless offensiveness that she felt sympathy for Focus's mother who, finding that

23

the world had intruded and that strange human adults had fondled her kittens, had eaten the better part of the litter and was starting on Focus when he was rescued by Aunt Irene's friend and thereafter raised on tinned milk dealt out by an old fountain-pen tube. She could see that you might consume babies when they were sweet enough to eat. At least you would know where they were. She worried about Kyril all the time, going about as he did in a world of fire and water, sudden concussions, cold steel and heights and depths, and taking so little care.

'They didn't expel her,' she said to Kyril in almost pleading tones. 'Your aunt wants her to see a little more of the world before she takes the veil.' Valentine, she could see, had no need of her protection. It was Kyril who put himself at risk, courting hostility and flirting with danger.

'Have a *croissant*, dear,' she said to Valentine, momentarily disliking her for causing Kyril to be unkind.

'No thanks,' said Valentine.

Aunt Irene glanced at her quickly. The girl was smiling—she didn't mind Kyril at all. And she isn't sad, thought Aunt Irene. She isn't in the least bit sad. She's quiet because she's *happy*. How extraordinary. Aunt Irene felt quite giddy with surprise and had to suppress a wish to reach out and touch Valentine as though she were a talisman. Perhaps it was the sun that made people happy. Her own people were mostly miserable. They wrote long glum books and sang glum songs and went on glumly about the extent of winter and the sound of the rivers freezing and the shortage of meat—not just the serfs who had had every reason to feel thoroughly depressed, but the rich and privileged. They worried about their souls and stared deeply and hopelessly into the depths of themselves. Well, that was how they had always carried on in the past anyway. It might be different since the upheavals, but Aunt Irene doubted it—circumstances did little to alter the nature of populations. They were probably worse, if the truth were known.

Kyril scowled. It looked as though Valentine wasn't going to play his game, didn't know the rules—didn't even know there was a game. Kyril was extremely fond of winning, and he always won, because he was prepared to go beyond the bounds of the acceptable; but you couldn't win against a person who wasn't playing. Valentine made him think of the rat who had strolled up from the river one day and sat on the wall, washing his whiskers and gazing disdainfully down at Focus mad with rage and hurt pride in the yard below. The neighbours had emerged to vanquish that rat, but he had slipped back to the river by devious routes, taking his time, when any proper rat would have been cornered, frenzied and snarling with terror.

Kyril was, in his own way, a very conventional man.

*   *   *

Reverend Mother took up her pen. She headed her letter 'The Feast of St Peter of Verona' and wrote . . . 'My dear Irene, Valentine is used to being thoroughly occupied . . .' She seldom mentioned Kyril in her letters except to say rather ominously that the Community was praying for him. Aunt Irene suspected that she had never forgotten the time when Kyril, as a child, had stuck a half-eaten apple, a lump of chewing gum and a deflated balloon on three of the spikes of the grille in the convent parlour.

*   *   *

The traffic was now in full flow along the Kings Road and the Embankment. The residential island that stood between and contained, as well as Dancing Master House, rows of artisans' cottages and a number of poet-haunted Georgian-type mansions overlooking the river shuddered a little.

There were occasional clangs and shouts from the yard at the end of the terrace where they stored drainpipes, and the sounds of old women putting things in dustbins.

Nevertheless, and despite the bomb damage which had shaken the foundations of many of these dwellings, even despite the close proximity of Peabody Buildings and the parish school, this was becoming a smart and desirable area and local house agents were smiling.

Aunt Irene's rich friends had told her she was crazy to buy a property in such a district, but she was never one to make that sort of mistake—and besides she liked it here. It was varied and lively and handy for Kyril's place of work on the Kings Road, where he traded in art. Then, too, there were a number of perfectly original people living locally: people who had simply grown like that without planning. Aunt Irene's conventional friends could tolerate the sight of these people, and described them as eccentric, but Aunt Irene went to their rooms and they came to hers. They ate and drank together—not only at tea time, which would have been just permissible, but at midday and in the evening, when gentlefolk dined with their peers. Aunt Irene was only forgiven because she had foreign blood and her distant connections were possibly quite extraordinarily grand.

Kyril went off to work wearing a velvet bow, and Aunt Irene trembled—not for Cassandra, his assistant, who loved him, but again for Kyril, since Cassandra's grandmother had put money into Kyril's gallery and if he were too

27

overtly awful to her grand-daughter she would doubtless take it all away.

'Have a care, *dorogoi*,' she called miserably. 'Oh, Valentine,' she said, 'I think you and my sister are so clever to cut yourselves off from the cares of the world.'

'So people say,' said Valentine, but she thought the sister of Reverend Mother should know better.

'You'll need some clothes,' said Aunt Irene.

'I have clothes,' said Valentine, not ungraciously, merely remarking upon a fact.

'Thin clothes,' said Aunt Irene. 'Summer clothes. Pretty ones. You'll get dreadfully hot in those black frocks and those thick black stockings.'

'This is not hot,' said Valentine.

'It *will* be,' insisted Aunt Irene. 'Even here the temperature sometimes reaches the seventies. We're going to have a good summer. I know. I have some new nylons in the fridge, you'll be much more comfortable . . .'

Valentine shook her head.

Aunt Irene regarded her. She was something of an artist herself and could seldom resist the temptation to gild the lily. She had no patience at all with the current view that functionalism was beauty and all applied decoration a sort of sin. When people spoke of art, buildings, coffee pots as 'contemporary', as though that were in itself a commendation, Aunt Irene sneered.

Valentine, she thought, looked stark—beautiful, but stark. 'You should wear flowers,' she said defeated.

'I will come shopping with you,' said Valentine, 'and carry the basket.'

Aunt Irene drew on her gloves and glanced down the street to see if Mrs Mason was coming. As she wasn't, she put the key under the boot-scraper. She bent to pick up some straying paper from the York paving stones that formed a tiny forecourt. In the middle she had planted a little magnolia, for which she cared as though it were animally sentient.

'Precious,' she said to it, in passing. 'Pretty precious.'

It responded with a nod of its smooth leaves.

Galaxies of small blue flowers like stars in negative lolled around on the paving stones, resting. The railings that once had guarded Dancing Master House had gone towards the war effort, and Aunt Irene hadn't replaced them. The man next door who let rooms had put a ramshackle fence in front of his property, and the old woman who lived in the basement had planted lobelia, pelargoniums, alyssum and London pride in the mixture of brick dust and cat shit that served as earth in the dinner-plate-sized garden. It was entirely Victorian in conception and execution, and Aunt Irene found it amusing: a piece of living horticultural history. She screwed up the bits of paper and

29

dropped them over the neighbouring fence.

Walking up the little street towards the Kings Road she wondered whether Valentine could appreciate the quaintness of the lace curtains and aspidistras that adorned most of the windows. At the corner a young couple had obtained building permission to restore a house to a single dwelling and were in the process of painting everything white. They were called Geoffrey and Jessica, or Julian and Jennifer, or something like that, and Aunt Irene didn't approve of them, although their presence undoubtedly raised the tone and property value of the street. They weren't subtle, she considered. They were youthful philistines—a depressing concept to Aunt Irene, who preferred to think of philistinism as the province of her smarter middle-aged friends. She could cope with them, and tolerate their invincible foolishness; but it was wearying to think that a second generation, precisely similar, was coming along.

The street didn't mean very much to Valentine—the brick-built houses, the pavements, the paint. There was a smell of bleach rising from a drain where an unusually hygienic old lady had been cleaning up the gutter, and the English scene became suddenly irrelevant. Valentine was home again, a little child—so small that feet and knees were as familiar to her as faces—and a girl had just sluiced down the verandah with *eau de javelle*, and three women in print dresses were sitting there at a low *rattan* table. And they were laughing. The garden was very close, alive with wind and sun, and all the creatures that stung and bit were doing something else that morning. She had thought she could see the pale silken waste of the sea which lay beyond the headland; so it must have been taken up and hung, briefly, as a backcloth to please her. She had been, considered Valentine, a very fortunate child.

Aunt Irene, glancing at her, thought she had never seen a human face so warm with pleasure.

*   *   *

Once in the Kings Road, Aunt Irene turned towards a newly opened coffee bar. She had an addict's passion for coffee—indeed her friends attributed her second marriage to the ability of the American Colonel to provide her with access to the real thing. Perhaps they were right. He had been tiresomely demanding for an American male, widely supposed to be an easy, generous creature. But then his ancestry was middle-European. He had seemed to come between Aunt Irene and the rest of the world like some great contraceptive, muffling her from all immediate feeling and experience, intervening between her and her friends, her interests, her beliefs. Nor had he cared for

Kyril. He had had to go. (Her first husband, Clovis, had been a Frenchman, until he'd died.)

'Do you ever think of marriage?' she asked, seating herself at a table.

'No,' said Valentine.

'You may be right,' said Aunt Irene, choosing one of the Danish pastries to which she referred as her *cream passionel*.

*   *   *

On the way home they passed the Bunch of Grapes, Major Mason visible through the open door of the public bar. Aunt Irene pointed him out to Valentine as one of the sights of the district.

Valentine said nothing, but Aunt Irene was suddenly visited by a sensation of the sea, very deep and green and cold, and shivered with the surprise she always felt when reminded that she truly possessed a psychic gift and was not a liar.

*   *   *

Mrs Mason was having a little snack when they got back home. She had put a lace tray cloth on the end of the oaken kitchen table and chosen a Spode plate and matching cup and saucer to place her biscuit on and drink her tea from. She behaved with grotesque politeness,

32

putting down her biscuit after each nibble and her cup after each sip and folding her hands in her lap like a child pretending to eat and drink.

Aunt Irene felt like pulling out the tray cloth and jumping on it. She ate because she liked eating, not as a demonstration of manners: sometimes she put her elbows on the table and waved her fork to emphasise a point. Now she took a biscuit and bit it with her right-hand teeth, keeping her mouth open and causing crumbs.

'There was someone here looking for you earlier,' said Mrs Mason, wiping her lips with a napkin. 'He said they'd written to you but you never replied. He thought I was you,' she added.

Aunt Irene's distaste at this ridiculous error was quickly dispelled by the unease that afflicts those who find themselves at odds with the Inland Revenue. Some minor official had been persecuting her for months with trivial enquiries about her means; but since she couldn't bear forms and had a profound conviction that her need of her own money was greater than the government's, she had ignored him. She felt the noble irritation of a fine spirit called from viewing the sunset to inspect the blockage in the kitchen sink. Her ancestors, she thought, would have had him boiled. In oil. Or, to be more culinarily precise, deep-fried. 'We'll have aigrettes for supper,'

33

she said, 'with fried parsley.'

'He said he'd call again later,' said Mrs Mason smugly.

' . . . followed by veal fillets,' said Aunt Irene flatly, as despair began to make itself felt. She would have to act the goat, she realised: the fluffy little person who couldn't understand the rules that men made. It was a role for which, though competent in it, she did not care. 'Did you say you weren't me?' she demanded of Mrs Mason.

'I said I was your housekeeper,' replied that lady, who had considered saying she was Aunt Irene's social secretary, torn between the wish to present herself in a classy light, the desire to drop Aunt Irene further in it and a disinclination to enhance her employer's social standing.

'Oh *good*,' said Aunt Irene. 'He'll think I'm Rothschild.'

'It's always as well to be quite open with these people,' said Mrs Mason.

Aunt Irene poured herself a scotch and spent some time looking desultorily and vainly for brown manila envelopes with windows in them.

*   *   *

Valentine went to church. As she came out she met a gaudy woman and the Parish Priest on the steps. He was a big old man and looked

34

ill—dappled, as the dead are. He seemed surprised at her appearance but expressed no interest. His mind was doubtless on the four last things.

'I know 'oo you are,' said the woman, gripping Valentine gently about the forearm. 'You're Valentine, stayin' with Aunt Irene. You tell 'er you saw Mrs O'Connor. Tell 'er Victor's got somefing for 'er. 'E'll be round 's'evenin'.'

Valentine went to watch the Thames flowing. She stayed for a long time, and then went into Holy Redeemer again on her way home.

The church was dark after the brightness of the street, cool and huge and infinitely reassuring. Going from the light into the enormous dark was, to Valentine, like going from life to death: a majestic enthralment, a vast elation, the calmness of eternal certitude—all could be had for the asking, simply by walking from the light into the dark. She went slowly round the Stations of the Cross.

*   *   *

Aunt Irene had finished her third scotch by the time the knock came on the door. She opened it with a bold and confident air, having decided to bluster rather than creep. This was the fault of the scotch.

'Mrs Wojtyla?' asked the person who stood on the step.

'What?' said Aunt Irene, thrown. 'Wojtyla' was the name of the American Colonel. Nothing wrong with it—she just found it impossible to remember that it was her name too.

'Oh yes,' she agreed after a moment, reflecting that this wasn't a good beginning: authority would certainly look askance on people who couldn't remember their own names. (She could actually remember the names of very few people and simply addressed everyone as 'darling'. This had contributed largely to her reputation as warm and slightly peculiar.)

'Come in,' she said, brightly, realising too late that she should have asked him his business. To compensate, she led the way downstairs and sat in the kitchen rocking-chair, leaving the young man to stand by the table. This was a mistake too—she had to look up to see his face.

'I saw your housekeeper earlier,' he said, putting his briefcase on the table.

'Char,' corrected Aunt Irene. 'She's the cleaning woman. The daily.'

'A nice lady,' he said, with what was possibly a touch of reproof. 'She gave me a cup of coffee.'

I bet she did, thought Aunt Irene. With the rat's-tail spoons and the Georgian coffee pot.

36

Slowly the tax man opened his briefcase.

*   *   *

Valentine wandered pensively out of the
church. The northern sun was warm this year,
meek and unobtrusive, with none of the
merciless candour of her own sun. The people
were turning different colours at its touch and
remarking on its power. Some spun round to
watch her as she walked, all in black, through
the little streets. There weren't many black
people in London. A few were being
encouraged over by the Government to
undertake tasks that the English were loth to
undertake themselves—on the tubes and buses
and in hospitals—and there had always been a
few at places like Balliol and the public
schools, but they were rare.

At the presbytery she met Mrs O'Connor
coming through the side door.

' 'Ere she is, then,' said Mrs O'Connor,
pleased. She was unusual in that she was
nearly always pleased to see a human being,
even the ones she didn't like, and she thought
Valentine was lovely. 'Bye, then,' she said to
the closing door. 'The Father's 'ousekeeper,'
she explained to Valentine. 'I give 'er an 'and
now an' then. 'Ot, isn't it? Then I don' s'pose
yer feel it like we do.' She chatted about
sunstroke on the way up the street.

As they reached Dancing Master House the

door opened and a young man came out. He was running. As they came level he stopped and stared at them and then turned and sped, hare-like, towards the Kings Road.

'What bit 'im?' enquired Mrs O'Connor. She watched him, puzzled. There was something about him familiar but out of place. He belonged in another context, like the film star who lived in the Boltons and was sometimes to be seen in a headscarf buying fish, or the lady in the Post Office who looked just the same but entirely different queuing up in her high heels outside the Odeon.

Aunt Irene emerged from her doorway and gazed after him. 'He's gone mad,' she said. 'We were just talking and he jumped up and shot out.'

'Caught short,' said Mrs O'Connor.

Valentine, who had been thinking about the dark, now lifted her eyes to the bright street. She looked unblinkingly at the back of the young man just disappearing round the corner. She had often seen people in flight—from dogs and ghosts and shadows and other people wielding knives. No one had ever been able to run fast enough. There was nowhere to keep running. Sooner or later the chase would end—over a wall, up a tree, in church or in blood.

Valentine was glad there was God. She knew there was, because she knew him well. And anyway, if there was no God, this terrible

38

world of pursued and pursuers would be Hell, and if there was Hell then there must be Heaven, since that was in the nature of things. And Heaven would have no purpose save as the residence of God . . .

'I don't know why you're laughing,' said Aunt Irene. 'I don't see anything to laugh about. Everything strikes me as rather worrying.'

'I'll make a cuppa tea,' said Mrs O'Connor. She made terrible tea, very slimy, strong and tooth-stripping, but there was no denying its restorative powers.

'If it does this to one's cups,' said Aunt Irene when Mrs O'Connor had gone home to make tea for her boys, 'what must it be doing to the lining of one's stomach?' She rubbed at the stained inside of the porcelain teacup. 'I can't be too rough,' she said. 'All its little gilt flowers will come off. They were designed for china tea. No one ever imagined Mrs O'Connor would cross their path.'

The world was upside down. On the whole this pleased Aunt Irene as much as it angered Mrs Mason. It was more interesting that way, but it was hard on the porcelain.

*   *   *

After dinner Aunt Irene confessed to Kyril that the tax man had been.

'I knew he would,' said Kyril, eating coffee

39

sugar.

'He went away again,' said Aunt Irene. 'It was very odd. He was going on about trusts and investments and alimony, and then he said he'd heard that a lot of people stayed here. That'd be Mrs Mason. So I explained about little Mr Sirocco and you and Valentine, and he looked very funny and then he ran away.'

'He thought you were keeping a common lodging house,' said Kyril. 'Bed bugs probably crossed his mind.'

Aunt Irene laughed suddenly. 'I thought he'd think I was terribly rich because of all the pretties, but he was rather sorry for me because everything was so old and I hadn't got any Pyrex dishes.'

'There you are,' said Kyril. 'He obviously thought the place most unsavoury.'

'Cheek,' said Aunt Irene, but quite blithely since he had, after all, gone away and she wasn't—as she had rather feared—repining in some fell dungeon in leg-irons looking forward to a bowl of bread and water.

*   *   *

At nine o'clock Victor arrived bearing a large parcel in his arms. It looked heavy.

Victor's family were totters and had a yard at Worlds End. They specialised in clearing out bombed houses, though as some of the brothers seemed not too adept at

40

discriminating between these and ordinary standing inhabited houses, one or two of them were currently putting in a spot of time at the Awful Place on Dartmoor.

Victor had early shown such precocious taste and talent for discerning things of worth among the rubble that he described himself, uncontradicted, as an antique dealer. He was a thin boy with a big nose and fair hair, and he wore neatly pressed trousers and white shirts, unlike his brothers who favoured padded shoulders and pointed shoes.

'Me bruvvers were clearin' out this 'ouse up west,' he said, ' 'n' they found these in the cellar. They were goin' ter sling 'em out, silly buggers, but I saw 'em in time. They're *old*.' He removed the flowered curtain in which his bundle was wrapped and lifted the lid of a wicker basket to reveal a collection of Delft manganese tiles. 'They'll've bin rahnd a fireplace, 'n' they'll've shifted 'em when the buzz bombs started comin' over.' He indicated the date on the newspaper between the tiles— dessicated newspaper like the leaves of many autumns gone.

Aunt Irene wondered briefly what calamity could have caused the owners of such things to forget about them. But then her whole house was furnished with the erstwhile belongings of the dead who had no further use for them. The dead were fortunate that their treasures had fallen into such good hands. Only

41

sometimes was she uneasily moved by vicarious sorrow: a box containing unworn baby boots, a walking stick, its handle shiny with years of use, family photographs—she hated family photographs. They made her feel that she might cry, and she never cried because she knew that once started there would be no reason ever to stop.

'I'll give you five,' she said.

'Ten,' said Victor.

'Seven,' said Aunt Irene.

'OK,' said Victor.

'Bring them into the kitchen and we'll lay them out on the table. And count them,' added Aunt Irene silently. She was aware that she had a bargain. Victor was smart, but he had a lot to learn.

The tiles were covered with the dust that bombs cause, gritty and grey and infinitely sad. Aunt Irene washed them carefully and laid them out in rows. They made up the sequence of the gospels.

'I fink they're religious,' said Victor, noting some haloes and a crucifixion.

'You'll have to ask Father O'God what order they go in,' said Kyril.

'You shouldn't call him that,' protested Aunt Irene. 'He's not well.'

The tiles were painted in a primitive ardent fashion by a committed believer who hadn't gone in much for the study of anatomy. 'Early eighteenth century,' surmised Aunt Irene,

42

wondering how she could set them off to best advantage. They could go round the fireplace in the further part of the drawing-room. The room would need redecorating to pick up the purple in the tiles—in a muted umber perhaps, with a touch of pink. Aunt Irene mixed her own colours, since the paint manufacturers eschewed all dark shades except for something known as Thames Green which was becoming too common.

Valentine began to arrange the tiles—the Annunciation, the Visit to Elizabeth, the Nativity . . . 'There are some missing,' she said.

'Damn,' said Aunt Irene.

The Flight into Egypt, John the Baptist in the Wilderness, a number of unfamiliar events that possibly the tiler had made up, the Crucifixion, the Ascension with Christ's shoes left on Mt Tabor and his feet just visible ascending into Heaven . . .

'I love that,' said Aunt Irene, 'I love it.'

She gave Victor a glass of whisky. 'Will you have a drink?' she asked Valentine.

'Thank you, no,' said Valentine, who was standing with a tile in each hand gazing uncertainly but with great concentration at the incomplete sequence on the table.

She looked like a girl assembling a family album, Aunt Irene realised suddenly. That loving care belonged to someone trying to remember whether that was the year George had measles, or whether the snapshot of Aunt

43

Ethel in the bathing suit should come before or after the picnic on Beachy Head. She looked like a lover smiling at reminders of the beloved, dreaming of his babyhood, his first words, his last words.

'*Noli me tangere*,' Valentine said aloud to the image of the risen Lord, shrouded in morning darkness, wounded hands outspread. God was fenced about with prohibitions because he was dangerous and extremely strange.

'There should be a sign in Aramaic,' said Kyril, peering over her shoulder, 'saying "Keep off the grass".'

'You should be careful,' said Valentine.

'It might be amusing,' said Aunt Irene, 'to set them out like a comic strip, all along one wall. But it wouldn't be right.' She gave Victor another whisky.

'That girl is boring,' said Kyril, though not until Valentine had gone to bed.

'Yeah,' agreed Victor.

'No, she isn't,' said Aunt Irene, thinking that Kyril and Victor had childish tastes—for sweet things, bright colours and loud noises; brief, unwholesome sensational things. Valentine was no more boring than a lake in the evening calm, and for the life of her Aunt Irene couldn't see that a lake in turmoil, disrupted by the winds, seething and flouncing, was in any way more interesting. Perhaps you had to be growing old, she thought, sighing, to appreciate this. She'd had quite enough of

44

storms and tumult and it would be very pleasant just to sit forever in mild stillness. It was remarkably pleasant just to sit in silence with Valentine.

'She never says anything,' said Kyril.

'I know,' said Aunt Irene. 'Isn't it nice?'

*   *   *

Mrs O'Connor called later. She had been Olde Tyme dancing and was wearing her ball gown. Aggie and Ted were in the van outside, she said, and they'd come to take Victor home.

'He's asleep on the *chaise longue*,' said Aunt Irene. 'It seems a shame to disturb him.'

'Passed out?' asked his mother. She liked Aunt Irene, who had no side. When Victor referred to her—as he sometimes did, since he was under the impression that he got the better of their bargains—as a silly ole see-you-next-Tuesday, his mother told him off for an ungrateful little sod.

Aunt Irene put the chain on the door. It would be unfortunate if Mr Sirocco should return, let himself in, go up to the bed he thought was his and get in beside Valentine. It was something Aunt Irene wouldn't care to have her sister hear about.

*   *   *

Next morning Valentine was up first. She

45

heard Victor leap from the *chaise longue* and run downstairs.

'Mornin',' he said.

Aunt Irene drifted in in her plum *kimono,* reaching drowsily for coffee. 'Your mother called last night,' she said. 'She'd been dancing.'

Victor was proud of his mother. 'She's awright,' he told them. 'Nuffin' gets 'er dahn. She was up all night, night afore last. There was coppers all over the place lookin' for Jimmy. They come down the skylight and up through the toilet.'

'Did they find him?' asked Aunt Irene nervously.

'Me mum was sat on 'im,' explained Victor. ' 'E was laid out under the mattress and me mum was sat on 'im wiv 'er curlers in, smokin' a fag. They come flyin' in an' she says, "Get out of a lady's bedroom at once, or I'll call the police".'

'I hope they don't follow you here,' said Aunt Irene.

'Everyfing you got from me is clean,' Victor assured her earnestly, 'clean as the driven. You got no call to worry.'

'I'm late,' said Kyril, adjusting his velvet tie. 'Last time I was late Cassandra took the morning off and went to the races.'

'You be nice to Cassandra,' warned Aunt Irene.

'The girl's a half-wit,' said Kyril. 'The other

46

day she called Matthew Smith "Mr John".'

'A mistake anyone might make,' said Aunt Irene amused.

The telephone rang as soon as Kyril had gone. 'Hullo,' said Aunt Irene; 'hullo, and hullo, and hullo hullo hullo . . .'

'Tell 'im 'e'll go blind if 'e does that,' advised Victor, struggling to get the better of a crumby *croissant* with jam on it, 'or screech down 'is ear 'ole.'

'I hate those,' said Aunt Irene, slamming down the receiver; 'they frighten me to pieces.'

'It's the workin' classes,' said Victor. 'They're ignorant, the 'ole lot of 'em.'

Victor had much in common with the late Führer. For instance, he thought that many problems could be solved by shooting a lot of people—in particular the working classes, homosexuals and the Royal Family (except for the Queen Mother, whom he quite liked). This would leave the upper and professional classes and Victor to run the country. And the Queen Mother of course.

'You can't tell the class of anyone by his breathing,' protested Aunt Irene, realising that if she had to have a heavy breather on her telephone she would prefer it to be a person of some standing in the community.

'Might've bin the Colonel,' suggested Victor.

'He's in America,' said Aunt Irene. 'He'd hardly bother to breathe across the Atlantic.'

She was horridly certain it was the tax man.

' 'Ope it's not Jimmy,' said Victor; ' 'e's bin actin' funny. 'E wuz floatin' up 'n' downstairs wiv a two-pound 'ammer, mutterin' the neighbours wuz abusin' 'im through the floorboards 'n' the wall, 'n' callin' 'im fings.'

'Were they?' asked Aunt Irene.

Victor shrugged. 'Dunno,' he said.

'Perhaps he was just drunk,' comforted Aunt Irene.

'Well, I'm off back to the Worlds End,' said Victor. 'I promised me mum I'd paper the landin'.'

He passed Mrs Mason on the doorstep. She ignored him. Tiredly she took off her hat and put it on the hall table, looking at her reflection as she did so. It was amazing how young she still looked, she thought, considering what she had to put up with.

'You look awful,' said Aunt Irene, truly concerned, as Mrs Mason came downstairs. The bags under her eyes were being joined by other bags coming up in a flanking movement from the sides of her face, and she was grey-white under her pancake make-up, which stopped short of the hair line and in front of her ears. The woman looked like something the Ancient Egyptians used to keep at their banquets to remind themselves that life wasn't just a bowl of dates and Osiris was hanging about at the end of the passage with his scales handy. 'Shouldn't you go home?' asked Aunt

48

Irene.

'I'm quite all right,' said Mrs Mason. 'I was up rather late. The Major—wasn't well.' She wished she could go home and lie down for a day or two, but the half-a-crown an hour Aunt Irene paid her was very necessary to what the Major called the kitty.

'Not well, my foot,' said Aunt Irene, when Mrs Mason had gone upstairs to do the bathroom. 'He was drunk as a skunk, is what he was.'

* * *

Valentine said nothing. When her sister Joan had drowned, her father had taken to drink like a saint to the sacraments, finding the world too terrible to bear, everywhere haunted by his daughter's absence. He incubated death and sustained it with rum. He cut himself adrift, returning once in a while to see if the world was still as cold and empty and agonising, and it always was; and then he would sink again into the green and silenced depths of drunkenness where he could neither hear nor feel and could see only dimly. 'T'ink of your liver, man,' the cook had implored him. 'Think of your responsibilities,' the priest had exhorted him, hinting further that this ungrateful and desperate behaviour could only serve to annoy God. Valentine had said nothing. There was really very little that the bereaved could say to each other, since trouble shared was trouble doubled. She contained her sorrow and observed her father doing the same: nothing but a vessel, an instrument for grief, denied all other purpose, so full was he. Of course he had died, his structure inadequate to the destructive force within him. Valentine had not shared the gloomy view the people had taken of his demise. To her he seemed to have fulfilled a role more nearly and precisely than others called to less harrowing modes of being. He would have come to himself in a dark garden, cool with the mists of morning, to hear his name being spoken. Of Joan she was less sure. Joan had been naughty—reckless and insouciant. She might be trapped in the light, the light that permits no shadow. And yet in the course of whatever passes for time in Heaven and Hell, all would be resolved, since the good deserve that the bad should be forgiven, the nature of goodness being to love.

*   *   *

The telephone rang at eleven. 'Huulloo?' said Aunt Irene, warily.

'Is that you, Irene?' asked the voice on the other end. 'You sound very peculiar. Are you pretending to be the butler?'

'Oh hullo, Diana,' said Aunt Irene, relieved. 'I'm not very well,' she explained, borrowing

50

Mrs Mason's mild ailment. 'I was up very late.'

'That's a pity,' said the voice. 'I was going to take you to lunch.'

'Oh, I *couldn't*,' said Aunt Irene, with what sounded too like enthusiasm to be polite. 'I think I have a migraine coming on,' she added in the interests of courtesy.

'That was Cassandra's granny,' she explained, shamefaced, to Valentine, who knew her to be in the best of health. 'I'm very fond of her but she's a frightful bore. She can't talk about anything but her wretched family.'

Aunt Irene knew all about pride of lineage and the lengths to which it could be taken. Her first husband, the Frenchman, had been given to boasting obscurely about his distant antecedents without disclosing precisely who these were. This had so irritated Aunt Irene, who had been a very inquisitive girl, that one day she had slipped him a mickey and gained the information that he was of the House of David. She had of course assumed from his pronunciation that he meant the painter of that name, and knew it not to be the case; but he had explained further that he was descended from Jesus Christ and Mary Magdalene who had run away together, crossed many peninsulas and capes and arrived in a tiny town in France where they set up house and had lots of little babies who grew up to be Merovingian kings. This frightful nonsense had disappointed Aunt Irene. Many

51

of her male relations had been Freemasons and some of the female ones Rosicrucians, so she was familiar with the inflated fantasy that feeds on secret ritual and borders on insanity. It was story-tellers again. They were such terrible liars and could never leave well enough alone. Especially the French.

A while later she wished she'd gone, because little Mr Sirocco returned to what he still thought was home. He called through the letter box 'Is anybody there?', which was one of his irritating habits. He had a key but was hesitant to use it in case it might seem impolite. Aunt Irene had the impression he was frightened of surprising her *in flagrante delicto*, which would have troubled her less than having to rise from her couch to let him in when he could have entered quietly and gone to read in the dining-room.

By the time he had followed her downstairs it was too late to tell him he must find other accommodation. He showed no surprise at seeing Valentine, partly because he was used to Aunt Irene's taste in people, but more because his nerves did not permit spontaneity and he put no trust in his instincts. If anyone else had been present and thrown up his hands and exclaimed, he would have done likewise. Lacking outside guidance, he merely nodded to Valentine and gave her the time of day.

Mrs Mason, adjusting her hat, announced that she was going now. 'There were some horrid old tiles in the kitchen,' she said. 'I put them outside the back door.'

'She does it on purpose,' said Aunt Irene. 'She was using a Rockingham sauce-boat as a sink-tidy the other day.'

Little Mr Sirocco's suitcase looked very out of place in the middle of the kitchen floor. Aunt Irene knocked against it as she went to retrieve her tiles. This offered her an opportunity to announce casually that his room was in new use; but she didn't take it, being uncertain of attaining the precise note of guilt-free reasonableness. The suitcase seemed to grow larger as they steadfastly ignored it.

Focus sat in the middle of the yard looking upwards at the pigeons circling the cross on top of Holy Redeemer as they spun into his line of vision. He chattered threateningly with his front teeth, his top lip receding. He seemed not to differentiate between the birds and the occasional aeroplane that passed.

'Silly, silly puss,' said Aunt Irene. 'What would you do if you caught an aeroplane? No feathers, no flesh. All bones.'

He took no further notice of her, lost in grandiose dreams of huge and joyful carnage.

'You would have loved the war,' said Aunt Irene. 'There were aeroplanes all over the sky.'

Silence fell. Valentine who was accustomed to a way of life in which speech was forbidden except at certain specified times or in emergency—a sister breaking a leg was not

53

required to wait until recreation before mentioning it—washed the cups and dried them. She felt no need to talk. It seemed to Valentine that there was very little to say, and that what there was had mostly been said. As far as she was concerned, silence was a perfectly suitable medium for the existence of living organisms.

Aunt Irene no longer felt like this. Valentine in silence was one thing, but with little Mr Sirocco present silence became another thing—a social embarrassment—and she was beginning to grow desperate. 'Did you have a good trip?' she said to him at last.

He responded in a squeak, having begun to think that he too might never again be called upon to use his vocal chords. He coughed and began again in a deeper tone. 'Very pleasant,' he said.

Silence. A distant rattle of drainpipes and the ever-rolling sound of traffic. Deepening silence that seemed to Aunt Irene to be taking on the hue of indigo and a jagged visible edge.

A pigeon, with the boldness that frequently accompanies lack of intellect, flew down into the yard where Focus was now asleep, a cat among the pigeons. It pecked about on the paving stones, and then walked into the kitchen.

Mr Sirocco screamed a bit.

'Hey,' said Aunt Irene indignantly to the bird. 'You go away. What's wrong with *you*?'

she asked Mr Sirocco, who was snow-white and trembling.

'I'm sorry,' he said. 'I know it's silly but I just can't bear them. They're horrible birds. In Camden Town they live on Irishmen's sick . . .'

'Do you mind,' said Aunt Irene. 'It's lunchtime, for God's sake.' Damn, she thought. Now she'd said it she'd have to feed little Mr Sirocco too, and once you'd fed people you had admitted responsibility, like saving a life.

'I have some fresh tarragon,' she said. 'I got it in Soho the other day.'

'I'll help,' said little Mr Sirocco, aware of crisis past. Baulked, the silence went away. It could bide its time. Eventually it would have the whole world to itself.

'*I* have to do it,' said Aunt Irene. 'It involves the peeling of soft-boiled eggs. You couldn't do that.'

'I could try,' said little Mr Sirocco.

'No,' said Aunt Irene. 'While you were trying you'd ruin the whole thing. I'd think you could see that.' She spoke more firmly than usual, being so displeased with the situation.

'Why don't you feed the cat,' suggested Valentine suddenly.

'Yes, do,' concurred Aunt Irene, crazing an egg shell with numerous taps on the draining board. 'There's no nourishment in watching birds.'

Kyril grinned when he saw little Mr Sirocco that evening. He leaned against the kitchen dresser and added a cigarette to his remorseless archaic smile. 'Well, well, well,' he said. There was something ominous in these apparently meaningless words. If Focus could speak, he might thus address a fallen bird.

Mr Sirocco shrank in his chair. 'Three holes in the ground,' he said, remembering an old school joke.

Kyril regarded him with coldly offensive incomprehension. Until now he hadn't really given little Mr Sirocco his full attention. At the time they had met he had been busy disengaging himself from his current mistress and had had plenty of scope for meticulous cruelty. Indeed he had been rather kind to little Mr Sirocco, since, in common with many unpleasant and neurotic people, he liked to prove to himself from time to time that he could be. It had been Kyril who brought him home when his previous landlady had required his room for her niece. Little Mr Sirocco had rather thought himself to be Kyril's friend.

'Where are you staying now?' asked Kyril.

'He's staying here, of course,' said Aunt Irene, noting with familiar distress the look of wicked pleasure on her nephew's lovely face. 'He's going to sleep in the drawing room until he finds somewhere to live.' It was done.

'You are silly,' said Kyril later. 'You haven't the courage of your convictions. He'd be gone now if you'd let me do as you asked.'

'That's all very fine and large,' said Aunt Irene, 'but he looked so pathetic.' He had reminded her of a puppy that had become inconvenient and was about to be given to a man who would take it to the country and abandon it beside the road. 'These things seem quite simple in the abstract—you need someone's room so you just tell him—but it isn't so easy when you see their face. You can't do it.'

'I can,' said Kyril.

'Well, you shouldn't be able to,' said Aunt Irene contrarily.

Kyril adopted his grown-up air, his masculine, sensible mien. He expatiated on the duty of one to oneself and pointed out that charity began at home. He explained that it wasn't kind to pander to people's weaknesses and it would be much more difficult for the invertebrate little Mr Sirocco to find his feet in the future now that Aunt Irene had encouraged him in his feebleness.

Kyril made perfect sense and was quite unconvincing.

'Anyway,' he said, tiring, 'you should've given him the old heave-ho, not the fatted calf.'

'I've given him the hint.' said Aunt Irene. 'He knows now he can't stay for ever.'

* * *

Reverend Mother wrote to Valentine. She headed her letter 'The Feast of St John Before the Latin Gate' and enclosed a picture of Our Lady of Perpetual Succour. 'I hope you have introduced yourself to the PP,' she wrote. 'He is a good man and will advise you well . . .'

* * *

At breakfast a few days later Aunt Irene apologised to Valentine. 'I'm afraid I opened your letter,' she said. 'Seeing my sister's handwriting I assumed it was for me. I thought she'd gone off her head, telling me to meet the PP. I've known him for years. I think it was that St John,' she continued, gabbling slightly, 'whom the Emperor Domitian boiled in oil— only he emerged unscathed, no more bothered than a scotch egg. It was when there were miracles still. But then the emperor was strange all round. He called a council of ministers to decide how to cook a walloping great turbot someone had caught. I suppose he'd lost faith in boiling oil. No frying tonight.' Aunt Irene paused. 'Oh, I *am* funny,' she concluded modestly.

58

Valentine was used to having her post opened. The novice mistress read all the postulants' letters before passing them on. It was one of the things that scandalised outsiders, so Valentine didn't mention it. She found it seemly. There were mysteries, but only the devil had secrets.

*   *   *

Mrs O'Connor called with a present for Valentine. 'Now it's getting 'ot yer'll need somethin' light,' she said. 'Jimmy found it in some 'ouse they were clearin' out. I got some more indoors. You can 'ave the lot if it fits.'

'Lovely,' said Aunt Irene, fingering the sea-green silk. 'Pre-war,' she opined.

Valentine refused the dress and Aunt Irene felt a melancholy kinship with Mrs O'Connor. She could have told her, if she'd asked, what Valentine's response would be.

'Pity, that,' said Mrs O'Connor. 'They won' look nearly so good on my Aggie. I c'd get a few bob for 'em,' she added thoughtfully.

Mrs Mason came forward. She picked up the dress, held it against herself and pirouetted dreamily. It was like the dress she'd worn to the last Tennis Club dance before war broke out.

'Ten bob,' said Mrs O'Connor coldly.

It was worth it, no one could deny that. Mrs Mason struggled with her conscience. A lot of

59

money which she could ill afford, but then she had so few good clothes. She bought it.

'Bleedin' waste on that ole bag,' observed Mrs O'Connor when her customer had resumed her duties. She pocketed the ten shillings. 'You goin' ter Benediction tonight?' she asked Valentine, ''cause I gotta see the 'ousekeeper at the Presbytery roun' about then. I c'd come wiv you.'

'All right,' said Valentine.

'You don't want a lodger, I suppose?' asked Aunt Irene. Little Mr Sirocco had gone to work enveloped in a miasma of reproach which it was impossible to ignore. She'd even offered to boil him an egg out of her undeserved feeling of guilt, but he'd refused it.

''Oo?' asked Mrs O'Connor suspiciously.

'Mr Sirocco's an awfully good tenant,' said Aunt Irene. 'Clean and reliable and . . .

'No fanks,' said Mrs O'Connor.

Mrs Mason, coming down for the furniture polish, was disgusted to hear this. She could herself have used a lodger's money, but her circumstances made it impossible, even if her pride had permitted; and the sight of that woman sitting down and refusing revenue, while she worked her fingers to the bone, made her quite ill. She would have liked to slap her common face, or pull her coarse black hair, but Mrs O'Connor's prowess in brawls was legendary in the district—and besides, Mrs Mason was a lady.

60

'I don't think it's right for me to clean the bedroom of a half-caste,' she said, as appalled and astonished as the rest of them to hear this remark hanging in the air. She stared round wildly, beseechingly.

'You are an unusually stupid woman,' said Aunt Irene. Mrs O'Connor was lost for words, and Aunt Irene was regretting hers, since chars were so hard to come by.

'I like cleaning,' said Valentine. 'I like polishing. I used to kneel down and put my ear to the floor when I was polishing it and listen to the mongoose chasing things in the cellar.'

'What things?' asked Mrs Mason tremulously.

'I'm not sure,' said Valentine. 'Snakes, I think. There were rats too.'

'Oh, I hate snakes,' said Mrs Mason. 'I'm perfectly terrified of snakes.'

'They weren't dangerous,' Valentine reassured her. 'Not as bad as the scorpions. The scorpions used to bite the gardener. He used to dance about and swear.'

Mrs Mason laughed. 'I can just see him,' she said, picturing a black man, loose-limbed and straw-hatted, leaping about in a garden full of scorpions and scarlet flowers.

'We called him Uncle Brown,' said Valentine. 'He had dozens of children.'

'Oh, the little darlings,' said Mrs Mason. Beaming piccaninnies eating crescents of melons thronged her mind.

'They used to play cricket with sticks and stones in the lanes,' said Valentine. 'My sister used to chase them.' She remembered Joan hurtling out of the verandah waving her arms, laughing and screaming.

'You have a sister?' asked Mrs Mason.

'She died,' said Valentine.

'You poor thing,' said Mrs Mason, comforted by the contemplation of another's sorrow. 'We all have our cross to bear,' she observed, and went back upstairs to polish the furniture.

'Oooh,' said Mrs O'Connor, still speechless. She came of a line of tinkers and had a deep personal dislike of prejudice. 'The ole . . .'

'She's a silly woman,' said Aunt Irene, rosy with embarrassment. 'I do hope you don't think . . .' She looked anxiously at Valentine. Berthe would be enormously displeased to hear that her *protégée* had sustained insult at her sister's house.

Valentine shrugged. She had seen evil before. She didn't like it, but it neither alarmed nor surprised her.

*   *   *

After Benediction Mrs O'Connor had a bit of a turn. She paused to light a candle for the conversion of the world before following Valentine to the door. Everyone else had gone. As she walked down the aisle she saw

62

Valentine in the doorway facing the altar, dark as a painted saint against the gilded evening, and just for a moment the light that outlined her outlined her completely and Mrs O'Connor could see light beneath her feet.

*　　　*　　　*

'What's it called?' Mrs O'Connor asked Victor over supper. 'What's it called when they float in the air? *You* know.'

'Eh?' said Victor.

'You're an 'eathen,' grumbled Mrs O'Connor. 'I just 'ope my poor ole mother doesn't know 'ow you bin brought up.' She cut into her black pudding, thinking hard and staring unseeingly at a picture of the Queen in her coronation robes looking young and bosomy, like a duck.

'I don' know what you're talkin' abaht,' said Victor sincerely.

While she was brewing a second pot of tea Mrs O'Connor's face cleared. Rising, she disappeared into a back room, whence came sounds of search. She returned with a sheaf of booklets published by the Catholic Truth Society.

'There y'are,' she said, slapping one open on the table. '*Levitation*. Tha's what it's called. St Joseph of Cupertino used ter fly in the air and sit in trees.'

'Go on,' said Victor. 'Pull the uvver one.'

'Everybody saw 'im,' said Mrs O'Connor. 'Bishops and mayors and magistrates. And there's St Martin de Porres,' she said, slapping down another booklet with an air of triumph. ' 'E was a saint—an' 'e's black.'

'You're nuts,' said Victor.

*   *   *

That evening when they'd finished dinner in Dancing Master House, there came a frenzied knocking at the front door.

'What on earth,' muttered Aunt Irene, rushing upstairs and fearing for her cherub's-head door-knocker. She flung open the door just as the street lamps were activated by the calloused hand of some remote artisan.

'Cassandra,' she said. 'What *is* the matter?'

The girl pushed past her and reached back to shut the door. She was frightened, as only the very young are frightened, glimmering and weightless with fear, each nerve and hair alert and separate. It seemed for a moment she could have flown with fear, and when she spoke her voice was high and twittering, like a bird's.

'There was a man,' she said.

'Good gracious,' said Aunt Irene. 'Where?'

'By the church,' said Cassandra, beginning to breathe again. 'He was just standing there.'

Aunt Irene shivered. She could see that this would be frightening. Most people did things

64

all the time, unless they were sitting at home, dropping off in their chair. There would be something alarming about someone standing doing nothing, in the dusk. 'But why are you here?' she asked. 'Were you coming to see me?'

'My grandmother sent me,' said Cassandra. 'She said you were ill and I was to bring you some grapes.'

'Where are they?' asked Kyril coming nearer.

'I must've dropped them,' said Cassandra, 'when I ran away.' She gazed at each of her empty hands.

'Perhaps the wolf ate them,' suggested Kyril. 'Little Red Riding Hood should be more careful.'

'Fox,' corrected Aunt Irene. 'It's foxes that eat grapes. They find them sour, and the little ones spoil the vines. Do run out, Kyril, and see if you can see them.'

'I'll go,' cried Mr Sirocco from the stairs. 'I'm not afraid.' He said that London since the war was more like Shanghai and no one was safe any longer. After a while he came back, saying his search had been fruitless. He repeated the final word.

'The man must've taken them,' said Cassandra forlornly. 'Granny'll be awfully cross.'

'I'll telephone her,' said Aunt Irene, who was rather blaming herself for the child's

65

fright. 'I'll explain, and I'll tell her we'll send you back in a taxi.' She was gratified to note, as she spoke to Diana, that her voice trembled as in one recovering from a migraine. She was, in fact, suffering from fear, for she *knew* that it was the tax man out there, watching her house from the shadows, and eating her grapes.

*   *   *

'It's not as though I could tell the police,' Aunt Irene confided to Mrs O'Connor in the morning, 'because naturally they'd be on the side of the tax man. I'm in a very difficult position and I don't know what to do.'

'I'll 'ave a word wiv Jimmy,' said Mrs O'Connor.

Aunt Irene couldn't see how a few convictions for burglary and GBH would qualify a person as a tax expert, and said so.

'Jimmy'll get some of the boys ter put the Frighteners on 'im,' explained Mrs O'Connor, amused at Aunt Irene's innocence. 'It's not right, 'angin' round outside people's 'ouses. It shouldn' be allowed.'

'I don't want any trouble,' said Aunt Irene nervously.

'You got trouble,' Mrs O'Connor reminded her. 'You got tax problems, an' you got Mr Sirocco.' She watched Valentine from time to time and speculated on the laws of gravity.

'I wish those pigeons would go away,' said

66

Aunt Irene. 'They make such a mess. Chase them, Valentine.'

Mrs O'Connor shook herself free of a vision of a girl soaring into the summer sky, a flock of pigeons scattering before her.

'Go away,' said Valentine, merely walking into the yard. Her feet made no sound.

'One got run over on the Embankment the other day,' said Aunt Irene. 'You never saw so many feathers. Don't you think . . .' she asked Mrs O'Connor, 'that if you could fly you wouldn't ever *walk* across roads?'

'Pigeons is thick,' said Mrs O'Connor.

Aunt Irene sighed. 'The Holy Spirit's a pigeon,' she said, wondering why. She found something infinitely melancholy in the mirthless chuckle of doves, and humankind had been told that the sign of the presence of the Holy Spirit was joy. She was being forced to realise that depression was upon her, and today was one of those days when the fact of death invalidated the whole of life. Taxes and death, death and taxes. Even the yellow sunlight made her think of old urine.

She wished she was like Valentine. Valentine, she thought, had nothing and yet had *hilaritas*, while she—with all her things and her people was suffering from *accidia*, that most debilitating malaise. Not fair, she thought childishly, watching Valentine looking at the sky. She was tempted to give all her goods to the poor and see what happened, but decided against it. There was no absolute guarantee that in return she would receive the contentment that characterised Valentine, and she'd feel pretty silly, shivering, naked in the world and *still* unhappy.

'I think I must give a party,' she said. Parties, like festivals, broke up the drear vista of existence from the cradle to the grave. Something to look forward to, like the next hostelry. A little warmth and diversion in the howling wilderness.

When her ancestors had travelled their huge estates—some were as large as small principalities—they had been forced to put up for the night in the hovels of peasants in their tribal villages. The headman of the particular Tartar, Chukchi or Bashkir clan would kick his animals, children and wives out of the single room, and the nobility would bed down amidst the straw and the smoke and have black bread and fermented mare's milk for breakfast. Sometimes they had journeyed so far that they found themselves in the lands of Shamans, or among people of no religion at all whose practice it was to do away with their old and infirm by spearing them, or throttling them with walrus thongs, or simply by sticking them on ice floes and booting them out into mid-river. The victims, it seemed, had cheerfully acquiesced in all this, even going so far as to entertain the neighbours to dinner before they died. Blow that for a lark, thought Aunt Irene.

68

The women, like Esquimaux, had been called upon to soften their husbands' sealskin socks by chewing them until their teeth wore right down to the gum. Great-great-uncle Grigorovitch had disappeared among these people together with all the expeditionary force he had led to see what they were up to. Nasty. Brrr.

It seemed extraordinary to Aunt Irene that she could feel such a sense of cold in the midst of summer. She took the fraying end of her depression and painstakingly followed it back to its source. Surprised, she found that it originated in the newspapers and not in her own circumstances. A woman was on trial for her life. She had shot her lover and accidentally wounded an innocent passer-by. Society was outraged. Aunt Irene felt better now that she knew what was worrying her, and was rather gratified to find herself capable of such disinterested compassion.

'Do you think she'll hang?' she asked.

'Oh yes,' said Mrs O'Connor.

*　　　*　　　*

'It's time something happened,' said Aunt Irene the next morning. 'Something pleasant. Nothing's happened for ages.'

Valentine was surprised to hear this. It seemed to her that things here happened every moment and she missed the convent where time was afforded the respect befitting one of God's more subtle creations. There it was carefully measured and used, but here the hours and days fell in upon each other in a meaningless jumble, like dominoes pushed over by a drunken hand. There was never enough time, since it was squandered so. Space too was here all cluttered up with Aunt Irene's acquisitions, until there seemed to be none left between her and her things, and no one had room to move.

It was like the Little Ease—luxuriously appurtenanced: cushioned and curtained and carpeted, and hence even more restricting than the bare bones of that cruel cage. She went to walk by the river.

Mrs O'Connor came in, breathless with hurry. 'The ole lady's died next door,' she announced. 'They've just taken 'er out in a bag. I told the bloke yer'd want 'er room for Mr Sirocco.'

Aunt Irene was overwhelmed with gratitude, astounded at Mrs O'Connor's promptness and thought. 'You're an angel,' she cried, kissing Mrs O'Connor's florid cheek. 'I don't know what I should do without you.'

Mrs Mason grinned without humour, maddening Aunt Irene, who at once embarked on her latest ploy.

'Professor English was here last night,' she said, gazing thoughtfully out of the window. 'He's extremely keen on Valentine going to

70

Oxford. He says she's superbly qualified and would absolutely definitely race away with a Double First. But then . . .' she went on, 'Maître Dagobert, who is cousin germane to my late husband, was here too, and he said she should go to the Sorbonne. With her gift for languages, he said, she was a natural.' Aunt Irene sighed. 'But Valentine is determined to go back to the convent. Lord Cockfosters and the Secretary of State for Animal Welfare were both here the other evening sitting each other out till the small hours—both on the absolute brink of proposing, but she showed not the faintest interest in either of them. Charming as always—courteous, friendly, but definitely not interested. Ah well . . .' She peeped surreptitiously at Mrs Mason, noting with malicious rapture the thread-like lines of jealousy and resentment, disbelief and rage that now lay like a web on the wretched woman's features.

'And Heinz saw her in the street the other day. You know Heinz . . .' she said to Mrs O'Connor. 'That brilliant producer who fled from Germany and made those marvellous films.'

'Yeah, I know 'im,' agreed Mrs O'Connor obediently.

'Well, he said she was exactly what he was looking for for his latest film. He would have signed her up there and then for the star part, but I had to tell him I was sure she wouldn't agree. I don't know when I've seen a man look so disappointed. He was prepared to offer her *anything*. I felt dreadful. The poor man had such a rotten time with Hitler. And now to be thwarted like this . . .' She sighed again, her head deeply inclined on her bosom and her hands limp on her lap.

Focus bit her. He was a straightforward and honourable cat, and his mistress's excesses always annoyed him.

*   *   *

Little Mr Sirocco moved out that evening, permitting himself to be rehoused as obediently as a guinea pig, and they all helped carry his cases.

'You must come to dinner any time you like,' said Aunt Irene, feeling positively fond of him now he was going. 'You'll like it here,' she said, gazing enthusiastically round his new room. It was small and drab with bits of greying cloth doing duty as doors on cupboards and alcoves. 'It's so cosy, and you've got your own little gas ring. You'll be able to make tea and boil eggs, and it's lovely and peaceful.'

The room was strangely quiet. The sound of drainpipes being thrown around seemed not to reach here, and even the traffic noise was muted.

'It's charming,' said Kyril, lifting a curtain

72

between thumb and finger and peering into a recess. It was quite empty. Victor and his brothers had cleared the room that morning and given the landlord ten bob for the lot.

'I'll give you a teapot and a cup and saucer,' said Aunt Irene, noting the bareness of the cupboard.

'I won't be doing much cooking,' said Mr Sirocco. He looked as though he might cry.

'No, well,' said Aunt Irene heartily, 'you won't need to. We're only next door.'

'You could always knock a hole in the party wall,' said Kyril as they let themselves out. 'Then he could pop in whenever he felt like it.'

Aunt Irene was defensive. 'He's a nice little man,' she protested. 'I'm sorry for him.'

Kyril adopted his elderly, caring air. 'He's seriously disturbed,' he said. 'You shouldn't ever accept responsibility for one in a trauma. He needs professional help.'

'Well, I like that,' cried Aunt Irene, indignant with her darling. 'It was you who stopped him going to that psychiatrist. You said . . .'

'I know,' said Kyril soothingly, spreading his hands. 'I know what I said. It isn't that I was wrong, you understand.'

'Oh no,' said Aunt Irene. 'No, of course not.'

They quarrelled a little as they entered Dancing Master House.

'He's one of those people,' said Kyril, 'who

73

once they go into analysis never never come out—which wouldn't matter if they'd keep it to themselves, but then they never talk about anything else. It gets to be a way of life, and they become extremely earnest and keep examining their motives and looking straight into other people's eyes, and yakking on about transference and ambivalence and complexes until you could murder them. It renders them entirely unfit for human society.'

'Kyril,' said Aunt Irene firmly, '*you* go on about that sort of thing all the time. You know you do.'

'But I'm so clever,' said Kyril tranquilly, 'and I'm not in analysis.' And in fact Kyril considered himself to be much much cleverer than the run-of-the-mill alienist. 'I knew it had gone too far,' he said, 'that morning when he cut the grapefruit the wrong way and went shooting off to West Hampstead for a quick consultation.'

'You only minded because he was boring,' snapped Aunt Irene.

'*Only*,' said Kyril, '*only* . . .' Kyril feared boredom above all else. When he was bored he thought he'd died.

*   *   *

To reassure himself Kyril popped into the Pheasantry, a pretty building standing back from the Kings Road. It was the site of a club

74

for interesting people: boring people were not allowed. It was full of people, all of whom were interesting though some were drunk. They stood at the bar, and those who could afford it were eating at small tables covered with check tablecloths and lit by candles in wax-encrusted wine bottles—a witty new idea from the Continent which had caught on rapidly. As Kyril entered, a well-known literary reviewer was biting the eyebrow of an art student, who wept a bit but made no real protest. She wore a circular red felt skirt with a tight belt, and ballet shoes. From the outer corner of each eye she had drawn a line in soft black pencil. This was called the doe-eyed look, and it was pretty irritating. Perhaps, surmised Kyril coldly, that was why she was being bitten; sometimes Kyril really detested girls. She wore scarlet lipstick and her hair was cut to resemble a coconut.

There were, as always, two sorts of homosexual—the rich and the poor. One of the rich now sauntered in wearing a camel-hair overcoat (into the sleeves of which he had not put his arms), a paisley silk scarf tucked into the neck of his shirt, and very expensive suede shoes. With hindsight, he was probably a Communist spy.

A nicer, poorer homosexual was entertaining a group with a scurrilous tale about a Member of Parliament, which none of the working or ordinary middle class would have believed, since those were the days when the English mostly thought their administrators to be incorruptible. He wore a tatty jumper and his bony wrists stuck out beneath the sleeves of his coat like a boy's. He was a talented but uninspired illustrator. So many things were against him: after a while he was to kill himself.

Kyril found to his surprise that these people were boring him. He lit a cigarette and looked round for someone to be rude to. With a sinking heart he realised there was no one worth the effort. He had another drink and admitted to himself that he was thinking about Valentine, and wishing she was here with him. She would set him off well. They would make a handsome couple.

*   *   *

Valentine was walking past the Pheasantry at that very moment. She had passed through London before but not noticed how full it was, how dirty: how impertinent the advertising hoardings with their exhortations to people to damage themselves and waste money on things to drink and smoke and put in their gravy. Everywhere there were invitations to commit foolish acts—Do this, Do that, Come here, Go there, Drink Bloggs's booze, Wear Gubbins's shoes. Unnecessary and intrusive when life was really so simple. It was sometimes extremely difficult, thought Valentine, not to be critical.

CHAPTER THREE

They hanged the woman who killed her lover. They hanged her for it. Quite early in the morning.

All through the day people gathered in groups in doorways and at bus stops, whispering, as though an evil event were imminent, not as though it had already happened. And it was a beautiful day.

'What will he do now?' begged Aunt Irene of all who passed through her house. 'The hangman. Is he on the train, reading the paper, going back to his wife and kiddies for tea?' She pressed her hands to her cheeks, appalled at the unchivalry of those powerful men—police, lawyers, judge, hangman who had done a tiny woman to death, and that for an offence that elsewhere would have merited merely a reprimand.

'She killed her lover,' said Aunt Irene, going on and on. 'Everyone wants to do that at some point. It's only natural. She just went too far. I wonder what the hangman's *having* for tea. Bacon and eggs, do you think? Plum cake? A glass of VP wine? I expect he likes very fatty bacon, fried in lard. With chips and ready-sliced bread and marge. I expect he has four

77

sugars in his tea, and cocoa for supper. With biscuits. He must be dreadfully constipated.'

'She killed a man,' said little Mr Sirocco, shocked at Aunt Irene's vehemence. 'A murderess.'

'Oh, nonsense,' said Aunt Irene. 'He treated her abominably.'

'I met a man the other night who'd been at Shrewsbury with him,' Kyril said. 'His housemaster told him he'd come to a sticky end.' He smiled.

'A gentleman,' said Mr Sirocco.

'So was the horrible person who put all those old ladies in acid baths,' said Aunt Irene who, in common with all other ladies of her age and class within a mile radius, had herself once been approached by this man with the offer of a gin and orange in the bar of the Onslow Court Hotel. 'It is not so, and it was not so, and God forbid it should be so,' she muttered superstitiously in the words of the unmasked Mr Fox, England's own Bluebeard. If it hadn't been for the curious circumstance that gall-stones aren't subject to the effects of sulphuric acid, no one would ever have known that the viscous liquid in the bath was the earthly remains of some English ladies, and the charming fellow would still be plying rich old dears with drink.

'So wicked,' she said, aloud.

Mr Sirocco gazed at her, confused.

'I mean the old ladykiller,' she explained

78

irritably, 'not *her*.'

Kyril was in an unusually good mood. He enjoyed drama and disaster and executions. It was a long time since a day at the seaside or a fall of snow would have served to excite Kyril. His tastes were strong and perverse and he was frightening his aunt very badly. She remembered him as a little boy with his big front teeth newly grown, pleased to see the Punch & Judy show—*That's the way to do it, that's the way to do it*—and felt the searing alarm of those who bring up children only to wonder where they have gone wrong.

'Execution is a terrible thing,' she said. 'There was once a Welshman who killed his father-in-law. He hit him with a shovel. He wouldn't have done it, but he'd been drinking. Anyway, they sentenced him to death and he was fearfully upset. They put him in the new gaol. Very modern it was, with an up-to-date treadmill and separate quarters for women prisoners . . .' She paused and regarded her audience. Little Mr Sirocco looked concerned and Kyril interested. She had been foolish to start on this story—Kyril would like it.

'Go on,' said Kyril.

'The women prisoners worked in the laundry,' said Aunt Irene, rather wearily, 'and there were holes in the ceiling with strings hanging down attached to the cradles on the floor above, so the women could pull them and rock their babies, if they cried, without leaving

79

the tubs and the mangles . . . Do you *really* want to hear this story?'

'Oh yes,' said Kyril.

'Do go on,' said Mr Sirocco.

'Oh, all right,' said Aunt Irene. 'Well, anyway this man was sentenced to death, as I said, and put in the condemned cell on the top floor—it was all very modern and labour-saving and he only had to walk along the corridor to a door that opened on to nothing, where the gibbet was. I don't know how they got him on to it. Perhaps they put the rope round his neck and gave him a shove . . .'

Kyril was fascinated by this speculation. 'There was a very original hangman once,' he told them, 'who wasn't satisfied with the tried method of tying the knot. He invented a new one and strangled umpteen malefactors instead of quickly breaking their necks as the old knot did.'

'Silly ass,' said Aunt Irene. 'I have no patience with people like that who want to do things their way even if they're wrong.'

'I think he did it because he enjoyed it,' said Kyril.

'Where was I?' asked Aunt Irene after a moment.

'He was walking along the corridor to the door that opened on to nothing,' said Mr Sirocco.

'Ah. Well, no—actually he wasn't. When the death morning came he'd barricaded the cell

80

door with his bench and trestle so that they couldn't get in. The governor, the minister and his wife and the hangman all implored him to open the door, but he wouldn't. It took them hours to break in. Then he struggled like mad all the way to the end of the corridor. It entirely ruined the tone of the occasion. But what I'm saying is—the point of the law should be that people agree to it, and if one party doesn't, then they should all think again.'

'Oh, that wouldn't do at all,' protested Mr Sirocco. 'No one would ever be punished then.'

'I think you're wrong,' said Aunt Irene. '*She* insisted on being hanged for what she'd done until the last moment when better sense prevailed. Too late. An awful lot of people go out of their way to be punished.'

'This is true,' said Kyril in his serious voice to Mr Sirocco. 'You should be aware of it.'

*   *   *

Victor was as upset by the hanging as Aunt Irene. He called especially to tell them so. 'They 'ate it inside when they does that,' he said. 'They bang on the bars wiv their plates an' some of 'em's sick. Our Jimmy went off alarmin'.'

'He's not in Holloway?' asked Aunt Irene, surprised.

'No, o' course 'e's not in 'Olloway, but 'e's

81

dead upset,' said Victor. ' 'S' not fair. I wouldn' 'alf like to see Ole Judge Owsyerfarver wiv a bag over 'is bonce.'

'Me too,' said Aunt Irene, wistful. 'But we never shall.'

'Come the revolution?' suggested Victor.

'The English don't revolt,' said Aunt Irene. 'In a manner of speaking, that is.'

'I've always enjoyed that joke,' said Kyril.

'I must plan my party,' said Aunt Irene, taking up her fountain pen from the desk, and hoping to fix her attention on more cheerful matters. She knew from long experience that her view of time was faulty and she found it very difficult to believe in future events unless they were happening tonight. A week hence was quite unreal to Aunt Irene. She had been late for both her weddings because of this failing; rushing to Worth for a dress at the last possible minute and scouring Paris for suitable shoes on the very morning of the day, while the *crème de la crème* fidgeted in Notre Dame. For her second marriage, at Chelsea Town Hall, she'd been even later, since as it was so close she'd assumed she had all the time in the world and there was no need to hurry.

'Can I bring Mum?' asked Victor.

'All right,' said Aunt Irene. 'Only not Jimmy.' She feared that wherever Jimmy went the police went also.

'Jimmy doesn' like parties,' said Victor. ' 'E's shy.'

Kyril didn't like parties either. He much preferred to keep his friends and acquaintances at arms' length in the Queen's Elm and the Anglesey. Their jokes and passwords fell slightly flat in people's houses, their manners altered for the better, they waxed boring—except for those few who were accredited geniuses and behaved disgustingly wherever they were, feeling it was expected of them, and they wouldn't be invited. Aunt Irene was far too fond of her pretty things to put them at risk from artistic drunkards, of whose work, in any case, she didn't think a great deal. She frowned as she began to draft her list.

Painters ranged over a wide class-spectrum, from dead common to the cousins of peers, and were mainly heterosexual. They would bring their wives and/or mistresses; but the writers of the day were almost uniformly homosexual, middle-class, middle-aged and sensitive, and not greatly given to the company of women. There were a few women writers, but as they were unmarried they were probably queer too, come to that. There really was an extraordinary shortage of suitable females—though what could you expect, Aunt Irene asked herself, if they persisted in hanging them.

'I can't think of any girls,' she said plaintively. 'It was never like this before the war. It's most odd. You'd have thought all the men would've been killed and there'd be

83

millions of spinsters like last time, but there aren't any girls at all except for art students. My numbers will be all wrong.'

'I c'd bring Aggie,' offered Victor generously.

'She'd do for the old person in the studio down the road,' Aunt Irene reflected. 'Only I'm not asking him. He takes up too much room and he's so old I'm always frightened he's going to drop dead on the spot—there's nothing more calculated to spoil a party. I don't think Aggie would enjoy it and she wouldn't get on with Diana at all.'

She had no fears for Mrs O'Connor who was confident and clever and played down her personality on these occasions so that the dumber, grander guests took her for some sort of servant and the bohemians took her for one of themselves, admiring her pectoral muscles, her coiled black hair and her high colour. Gypsies were still popular with artistic people and Mrs O'Connor was a bold bright creature.

'I'll have to ask Rosemary,' said Aunt Irene. Rosemary was Kyril's most recently discarded mistress. She was behaving well and bravely, but they had heard from friends that she was still deliriously unhappy.

'God no,' said Kyril. 'She'll think I'm groping for a reconciliation.'

'I can't help that,' said Aunt Irene; 'she's a girl.'

'Well, if *she* comes, I'm not,' stated Kyril.

84

'You're so inconsiderate,' said his aunt. 'You only ever think of yourself.'

'I'm thinking of Rosemary,' said Kyril mendaciously. Actually the thought of Rosemary made him sick. The memory of the smell of her tears and the touch of her soft hands filled him with murderous repugnance. Remembering sexual intercourse with the poor girl made him feel like a vicious but violated child, and his clear awareness of this did nothing to improve his opinion of her.

'She was so sweet,' said Aunt Irene, in benevolent mood since it was plain that Kyril didn't hanker after this erstwhile bedmate.

'Oh God, she was,' said Kyril, shuddering, 'so *sweet*.'

'Nothing wrong with sugar . . .' said Aunt Irene, and at that Valentine rose and left the room. There was something odd in the manner of her rising and leaving which Aunt Irene discerned at once. 'Valentine's upset,' she said.

'All that chat about sugar,' said Kyril nonchalantly. 'Her grandpappies probably spent all their time chopping down cane.'

'She doesn't seem to me a particularly deprived sort of girl,' said Aunt Irene. 'I don't believe they did that. I think they made other people do it. Perhaps that's why she minds.'

'You're a hypocrite,' said Kyril, pleased to be offensive after the recent reminder of his immaturity and inadequacy. 'You think you have this tenderness for the underprivileged,

85

but you only like the exceptional ones—successful crooks like the O'Connors—'

'Pardon,' said Victor.

'—exquisitely lovely slave princesses like Valentine, hanged murderesses. You have no time for the mediocre. Ordinary decent bank managers, policemen, politicians, the royal family leave you cold.'

'You may be right,' said Aunt Irene, faintly flattered. 'What about Mr Sirocco, though?' she asked, undecided between the natural desire to demolish her nephew's argument and the rather pleasing image of herself as patron of the astonishing.

'You just got landed with him,' explained Kyril. 'You're not a cruel woman and you can't say no. You wouldn't've chosen him.'

'True,' agreed Aunt Irene, nodding gravely. 'Very true.'

'Speakin' o' fievin',' said Victor, smiling collusively, 'me mum's got some Nottin'ham lace curtains for yer. Genuine. Lovely, they are.'

Aunt Irene narrowed her eyes, considering. Looped swags of lace at the windows? A green plush tablecloth with bobbles? Lilies? A samovar? She could see herself, a character from Russian literature, tragic and bored behind the lace curtains. The vision somehow lacked appeal. Something about it was grimy—dirty fingernails and greying wrinkles, a general lack of sparkle and a weighty sense of tedium. 'I'll have them,' she said, 'but I don't know if I'll hang them.' Part of the trouble was that some of the neighbours still had Nottingham lace curtains adorning their windows in perfect seriousness. People might not see the joke.

'Make a smashin' weddin' dress,' said Victor with the air of one smitten by brilliance.

They looked at him in silence.

'I have no plans to get married again,' said Aunt Irene at last, 'but I'll think of something.'

She thought of the sea. It was the mention of lace that brought it to mind, and she thought of northern seas, the tall grey breakers of puritan grey, incongruously collared in a cavalier exuberance of foam, rearing drunkenly to shore and collapsing on the beach. She could feel the clutching clamminess of seaweed and hear the cash-like clink of pebbles handled roughly by the dying waves. But I like the sea, she told herself, depressed by these images of debauchery and greed. The seven seas have been good to us, putting themselves between us and those who wished us harm. How dreadful it would be if it were possible to quarter the earth on foot. No one would be safe, ever. Great hostile hordes, already vile-tempered because of their blistered soles and aching tendons, would march round and round raping and pillaging—and nowhere to paddle, nowhere to roll up their dusty trouser legs and soak their weary limbs. There wouldn't be any rain either, Aunt Irene told herself scientifically. The world would be a wilderness of dust.

Despite its ambivalence (it would as soon send you down to Davy Jones's locker as bear you safely from hither to yon) there was something reassuring about the sea. Although moon-dragged, it was not girlish, not captious. It was mature, thought Aunt Irene—not terribly nice or terribly kind; severe, in fact—having no scruples in disposing of those lovers of whom it had grown weary, but on the whole, good in a crisis. Good at distancing warring factions, like a sensible mother. Or an Aunt . . .

'You seem very remote,' said Kyril.

'I was trying to think of excuses for the sea,' said Aunt Irene.

'I don't think it needs any,' said Kyril. 'It's much older than us. We all came out of it—funny little see-through things with monocular vision and whiskers.'

Victor observed them, fish-eyed. 'Wha'?' he demanded.

'It's a theory,' explained Aunt Irene. 'Some people seem to imagine we all crawled out of the ocean some time ago as teeny little maritime bugs and then evolved into us.'

'I fort it wuz monkeys,' said Victor, for the theories of Darwin had already by this time percolated right down through society to the very sediment.

'It was probably monkeys next,' said Aunt

Irene. 'After the reptiles and so on. The little squishy things turned into fish, the fish into reptiles, the reptiles into birds, the birds into . . .'

'Monkeys,' said Victor derisively. 'I s'pose that's why they 'ang abaht in trees.'

'It's extremely difficult to explain,' said Aunt Irene rather pompously, for she knew that if she actually understood this theory it would be easier to propagate. The fact that she didn't believe a word of it herself was irrelevant at the moment. She wanted to convince and educate Victor and wipe that naughty look of amused and superior contempt off his face. It was suitable, she thought, for persons of her background and education to dismiss as potty as many theories as they liked, but it was very annoying when the unlettered did it.

Aunt Irene really inclined to that simplest of all views: the one expressed so cogently in the book of Genesis, which explained everything with appealing clarity. This was the only view that explained, for instance, mayonnaise. It was patently absurd to suppose that mayonnaise had come about through random chance, that anyone could ever have been silly or brilliant enough to predict what would happen if he slowly trickled oil on to egg yolks and then gone ahead and tried it. An angel must have divulged that recipe and then explained what to do with the left-over white. Meringues—there was another instance of the exercise of superhuman intelligence. To Aunt Irene the Ten Commandments seemed almost insignificant compared with the astonishing miracle of what you could do with an egg. As the angel had left in his fiery chariot he must have added, 'And don't forget omelettes, and cake and custard and soufflés and poaching and frying and boiling and baking. Oh, and they're frightfully good with anchovies. And you can use the shells to clarify soup—and don't forget to dig them in round the roots of your roses', the angelic tones fading into the ethereal distance.

It was obvious therefore that the egg had come first. There was something dignified about a silent passive egg, whereas Aunt Irene found it difficult to envisage an angel bearing a hen—which, despite its undoubted merits, was a foolish and largely intractable bird. The concatenation of chickens' wings and angels wings would have had about it an element of parody which would have greatly lessened the impact of the message.

There must have been three eggs, thought Aunt Irene, going into details. One to eat then and there, and two to hatch—a boy and a girl. It was quite possible to hatch an egg in a human arm-pit—it had been proved on various American campuses and went with swallowing live goldfish and putting ferrets in your trousers.

'Why are you looking like that?' asked Kyril.

'I was wondering why people put ferrets in their trousers,' said Aunt Irene.

'*Thanatos*,' said Kyril. 'An illustration of the death wish.'

'What I wish,' said Aunt Irene, 'is that you'd never read Freud. It's had a very leaden effect on your conversation.'

*　　　*　　　*

Reverend Mother opened the drawer of her desk and stared thoughtfully for the hundredth time at what lay within. She closed the drawer and sat back in her straight, hard chair, her hands folded on the surface before her. Now she closed her eyes.

It was the previous autumn and the year had grown richer as it had grown older. September pressed like gold-leaf on the land until all things were gilded and roseate and glowing like glory—trees and garnered fields and the sedge by the river.

She could hear herself speaking that evening at Recreation. 'I think it is time,' she had said, smiling for the pleasure she would give the nuns, her children, 'for us to harvest the apples.'

And the next morning the able-bodied had gone forth into the orchard, their gowns kilted, their sandals strapped securely to their feet— with baskets and ladders and hooked sticks. The younger nuns had gone up and down the ladders with their veils pinned so as not to catch in the branches, and the older nuns had gathered the windfalls from the golden grass.

Then the youngest nun had stood back and clasped her hands together and looked upwards and said disconsolately, 'Oh, dear Reverend Mother, the best apples are right at the top of the tallest and oldest tree and we can't reach them.' And she had replied: 'No matter, my daughter, the birds will enjoy them, and we have a great many for ourselves.'

But the youngest nun, who hadn't yet had much practice in renunciation, had sighed, 'It seems such a *pity*'. And Reverend Mother herself had thought it faintly galling to see the scarlet and crimson fruit hanging in such perfection beyond their grasp.

Then they had turned and carried their baskets back to the convent store-house and Valentine had come last. And when she joined them her basket was full of the largest, brightest, most flawless apples; and Reverend Mother had gone back to the orchard and stood under the tallest and oldest tree and gazed upwards into its branches, and it was entirely bereft of fruit. Its leaves would be coming off soon as well, but it didn't seem to mind.

That night the whole world had smelled of apples. The drawer of her desk still did. Inside it was a large bright flawless apple as crisp and fresh and gleaming as when it had been picked all those months ago. She had another look at it and willed it to wither. Until it did Valentine could not return, for there was nothing, absolutely nothing, as tiresome, exhausting and troublesome as a fully functioning thaumaturge in a small community. The more volatile nuns would get over-excited and the steadier ones worn out with coping with the vast crowds of sightseers who would jam the narrow lanes and ruin the crops of the neighbouring farms, and throw crisp packets and bottles into the river and the hedgerows, and strip the convent of stones and the orchard of wood for relics. There would be journalists and film cameras and charabancs and all manner of inconvenience. The bishop would be displeased, and no one would get any sensible work done at all.

In the mean time everyone was missing Valentine, and although Reverend Mother knew that her nuns trusted her, she also knew that they didn't understand why she had sent Valentine away. She wasn't too clear about it herself. All she knew was that the Lord in his infinite subtlety had given her this apple as a sign, and that only when the beastly thing conformed to the laws of nature—which after all were also God's laws—could Valentine come back. It was a reversal of the usual plot which decreed that heroines should go out searching for golden globes of this and that.

How the vulgar loved portents, prodigies

and the untoward. Only the religious knew how embarrassing they could be—and quite beside the point.

*   *   *

Next morning in Dancing Master House there was another empty telephone call. Aunt Irene smashed down the handset with absolute disregard for the possibility of breakage.

'Steady on,' said Mr Sirocco, considerably startled and quite put off his honeyed toast.

'I-just-wish-I-could-get-my-hands-on-whoever-does-that,' remarked Aunt Irene snarling and speaking through clenched teeth.

'Valentine,' she called sharply and stopped, puzzled.

'Yes?' said Valentine, turning from the sink.

'Nothing,' said Aunt Irene. She could hardly say 'That call was for you', since the caller had spoken never a word. But it was, she was sure. She was quite certain that the speechless person wanted Valentine. She was also still certain that it was the tax man; so the whole thing was thoroughly bewildering. 'I feel as though my brain cells were drying up and dropping out like dandruff,' she said. 'The reason totters.' The day seemed suddenly sullied as though evil had passed over like fog, leaving scum on all her shining things. She whipped the counterpanes off the beds and gave them to Mrs Mason to take to the

94

laundry on the Kings Road on her way home, and she told Kyril to watch out for the window-cleaner.

Kyril was himself in a filthy mood. Little Mr Sirocco, who claimed that the bath next door was deficient in enamel and that the geyser was unsafe, was in the habit of taking his bath in Dancing Master House. He had been in it this morning when Kyril wished to be. Kyril had kicked the door and used language.

'There's no need to behave like that,' Mr Sirocco had said, sidling nervously out of the bathroom with his sponge-bag and towel, his hair all dark with damp.

Mr Sirocco had stepped on Focus's tail, purely out of nerves, earning himself a look from Aunt Irene and eliciting from Focus the unique, inimitable sound of trodden cat, and it seemed that Mrs Mason had broken her fast on a bowl of vinegar.

'*Gospodi*,' remarked Aunt Irene to herself. 'I shall go to church.' She pulled on her gloves and a pink hat—she always wore pink or shades of purple. '*Porphyrogenita*,' she said.

Mrs Mason, rolling up the sleeves of her cardigan, thought Aunt Irene looked like one of those backyard hydrangeas. It was significant that she had so many clothes—not all of them pre-war by any means and nothing Utility. Mrs Mason was absolutely convinced that Aunt Irene had traded with Mrs O'Connor in black-market clothing-coupons

95

throughout the Duration. Her face grew lined and set with jealousy and she wished the tax man would come back—she could tell him a few more things.

'I like your hat,' she said in a nasty voice.

'What's wrong with my hat?' muttered Aunt Irene automatically, '. . . the cook admires it.' She too was thinking of the tax man. There had been no manila envelopes for some time—in itself a sinister circumstance. She peered up and down the street for lurkers. It was undeniable that her house did not offer the appearance usual to the houses of single gentlewomen. It looked too prosperous for one thing, since prosperity had not yet been rehabilitated as synonymous with good taste. Mrs Mason was far from alone in her prejudices. Then there were always so many people coming and going: the thought of brothels must sometimes cross the mind of any normally prurient observer. There were Kyril and Victor and Mr Sirocco, Cassandra in and out on errands for Kyril. Now there was Valentine—*toute belle*—and Mrs O'Connor, who at her best mightily resembled the Whore of Babylon. And Mrs Mason—but no one, no one, could take Mrs Mason for a *fille de joie*. Aunt Irene laughed quite loudly at the mere thought, cheering herself up.

*　　　*　　　*

Aunt Irene's devotion to God—or *Bog*, as her ancestors had doubtless referred to Him—was rewarded at lunch time, for she was still crawling round the sacred floor when a terrible thing happened.

Major Mason lost his pocket money. He had paid for his first few drinks with his loose change and then felt vainly in his wallet for the note that should have been there. The barman inexcusably refused him credit, and Major Mason gave a staggering leap on to the Kings Road, like a small bull entering the bull ring. He swung his head from side to side before remembering where he'd find the picador, and then set off down the side streets to Dancing Master House.

Mrs Mason polishing the front door brasses saw him coming round the church and shrank, smiling with terror into the shadow of the hallway. He wasn't, as yet, at all incoherent, and he berated her fluently for her meanness, incompetence, dishonesty and idleness. He went on to describe her physical appearance and made passing reference to her family, finishing up with a crystalline description of what he thought of a woman who did other women's washing, like some horrible *dhobi wallah*.

Of course all the noise attracted the attention of Mrs O'Connor, who was with the housekeeper tidying away some things in the presbytery.

'Yer shoulda' smacked 'im in de mahf,' she advised, intolerant of Mrs Mason's fearful and shamed demeanour. 'You let the buggers get away with carryin' on like that—nex' thing yer know they're crackin' you one with the coal scuttle. You shoulda' *bashed* 'im.'

'Oh no,' said Mrs Mason, still, for some reason, trying to smile. 'He's all right really.'

This was clearly such arrant nonsense that Mrs O'Connor and Valentine could think of nothing to say.

'Before the war,' said Mrs Mason, 'before the tragedy, he was such a gentleman, so charming.'

Mrs O'Connor, thinking that the Major would always have evinced about as much urbanity and charm as your average Orangeman, made a noise expressive of disbelief which she thoughtfully disguised as a belch.

'Cup of tea,' said Valentine. 'In the kitchen.'

' 'Ave plenty o' sugar,' said Mrs O'Connor. 'You look 'orrible.'

They made rum from sugar, thought Valentine. But her father had never got drunk like the Major. Never got drunk at all until the Scheme and the death of Joan.

*   *   *

The Scheme had been thought up by the most prominent islanders with the idea of

98

encouraging tourism after the war. They had offered a prize for the best essay on the subject of a Tropic Isle, and rather than pay the exorbitant sums demanded by the English national dailies, they had put the details of the competition in many small local papers. The prize was a holiday on the island for a family—numbers, recklessly, unspecified. A South London civil servant called Stanley had won it and taken with him his wife Jill, her mother and his sister; and Joan—never a girl to do things by halves—had drowned the lot of them and herself into the bargain. Only Stanley, although a non-swimmer, had managed to cling to a piece of flotsam and drift ashore, where he was fished out by a lady on a lilo.

Joan, Valentine knew, would have denied direct responsibility for this mishap. She had never before caused a fatal accident: it was just that she enjoyed speed above all things and had never been able to resist frightening the life out of people—the charitable called it *joie de vivre*. Time and again Joan had sneaked down to the jetty, started the old motor boat (which did not belong to her) with a bent hairpin and shot out to sea followed by the recriminations of the boat's legitimate owner, who was usually to be found dozing under an upturned rowing boat on the warm sand. She would return followed by the curses of people in smaller boats rocking wildly in her wash. But she'd never made anyone fall in before, and even if she had, all the islanders could swim. This time, hindered by the savage attack of a normally pacific sea bird which had run out of patience with her, she had lost control of her stolen boat and collided dramatically with the admittedly leaky old thing in which Stanley was taking his women for a spin. With a huge crash and a vast splash the two vessels had sunk swiftly beneath the previously calm waters. The sea bird, still feeling that it hadn't settled the score, had beaten Joan with its wings and struck at her with its beak until she could swim no more and had gone to the bottom with the other ladies.

Stanley, mad with grief and outrage and dripping wet, had vowed vengeance on everyone in sight. The superstitious people had murmured feelingly against Joan and her boating style and glanced threateningly at Valentine and her father, but Stanley on his return home alone had confined himself to sending cuttings from newspapers to all at Hibiscus House. They were taken from the same local newspaper, and they dealt with aspects of Stanley's and Jill's amateur ballroom dancing successes—tragically cut short by Death. 'They were very popular members of the Lambeth Ballroom Dancing Association', 'Jill's mother made her frocks and her sister-in-law did her hair', 'Jill and Stanley had won the trophy for the Valeta for the third year running'.

The last cutting was from the obituary column and consisted of a short home-made poem, so awful that Valentine's father had laughed for the first time since his darling died. 'Joan would like that,' he'd said and grown instantly grave again.

No letters had come with the cuttings, and no signatures. Stanley had obviously imagined that somehow the official reminders of the loss he had suffered would bring home to the family of the person responsible something of his own grief and bereavement; but they didn't. All the cuttings made the cook laugh. He'd mince round the kitchen holding his apron between finger and thumb, being Stanley and Jill by turns, and his performance always ended with a spirited impersonation of several people drowning. 'Hell, man, you leggo ma dancin' feet. Glug Glug, etc . . .'

Valentine had found Stanley's humourless emanations of vengeful hatred quite unmoving. He was wasting his time and his life wishing he could punish a dead girl, willing to visit Hell to find her, prepared to creep like a snake over Heaven's boundaries, wriggle through the fields of asphodel to seek her out and bite her immaterial leg with his immaterial venomous teeth. As the cook observed, 'He sick, man'.

Her father was sick too. He explained that he had lost not one daughter but countless daughters. Joan the first-born baby and the

101

baby wailing in the night; Joan learning to smile and Joan walking; the wicked child laughing at him from the forks of trees; and the beauty, the girl with no sense of danger or decorum—up in the hills with the sorcerers dealing darkly with chickens and stones and sticks, silent in the darkness, all gaiety gone with the cuckolding sun which had slipped away to warm alien people. Joan and the witches behaved badly in the night. Impotent and jealous, they wrought spells and sought potions to console themselves for such gross betrayal. That was the girl who had brought them all to death. All the Joans had drowned in that cruel thoughtless girl speeding round the bay in the old motor boat, running down tourists, when everyone had supposed her to be quietly sitting at home in Hibiscus House.

Joan with her living, streaming hair sinking into the depths of the bay . . .

*　　　*　　　*

Aunt Irene, arriving back, could smell the sea as soon as she opened the front door.

There were several pigeons tripping round the backyard, their toes turned in.

'I wish you wouldn't feed the pigeons,' she said to Mrs Mason, before realising that Mrs Mason should have gone by now, and also that she appeared deathly ill.

'I don't feed them,' said Mrs Mason. 'I don't
102

like them.'

Kyril fed the pigeons. He gave them peanuts for reasons of his own.

As Aunt Irene walked to the door to scream at the birds, she stared at her cleaning lady, who sat in an attitude of despair, her hands drooping between her knees and her head bowed. Aunt Irene looked interrogatively at Mrs O'Connor, who smiled and winked reassuringly as one who will tell all later.

'Go away,' said Aunt Irene very loudly, taking off her gloves to clap her hands. The pigeons ceased their pecking, cooing and strutting, and flew off to wheel about the cross on top of Holy Redeemer.

'I've never *seen* so many pigeons as we have this year, and they've forgotten some of their horrid feathers . . .' began Aunt Irene. She got no further, as a disturbance began in the street. Even in the basement kitchen they could hear it. Mrs Mason shuddered and crumpled.

'Flippin' Ada,' remarked Mrs O'Connor, who was first on the scene.

'What is it?' gasped Aunt Irene, toiling up behind her and peering out of the front door.

The Major was coming down the street, bowling like a hoop and howling like a wolf. He rolled along the gutter smiting the kerb as he spun, shoulder, hip and thigh, springing now to his feet, now flinging himself backwards in a somersault, shrieking the while

103

that the devil had sent his fiends to fetch him.

'The *loup-garou*,' said Valentine.

'DTs,' said Mrs O'Connor. She leapt down the steps and grabbed him as he came opposite Dancing Master House. ''Old 'is legs,' she directed Aunt Irene. 'Valentine, nip roun' Peabody Buildin's and look for a pram, 'n' when you've foun' one fin' out 'oose it is and make 'er give you the baby's orange juice. Tell 'er it's a matter of life 'n' deaf. 'S the only fing,' she told Aunt Irene as they grappled with the writhing foaming Major. 'Concentrated orange juice's the nex' bes' thing to scurvy grass, 'n' we got no scurvy grass.'

'Mango juice is good too,' said Valentine, 'but we've got no mangoes.' She sped towards Peabody Buildings.

'I 'ope no silly fricker's sent for the Ole Bill,' said Mrs O'Connor looking round apprehensively. 'We c'n do without them. Shut up, you silly ole sod,' she directed the Major. 'Siddown.'

'What's he saying?' asked Aunt Irene.

''E says the sky's black wiv devils,' translated Mrs O'Connor after a moment.

'But they're pigeons,' objected Aunt Irene. 'Filthy dirty pigeons.'

'They *look* like pigeons,' corrected Mrs O'Connor, briefly lifting a hand from the Major to cross herself with it.

Aunt Irene looked up at the sky

involuntarily. 'Surely you don't think they're devils?' she asked.

'I'm not sayin',' said Mrs O'Connor guardedly. 'Only some funny fings 'ave bin 'appenin', 'n' all I'll say is—devils don't bovver in this manner in the ornery way 'cos everyone 'ere's wicked enough already. They mos'ly spend their time in monasteries temptin' monks. They're idle, devils are—they don' do nuffin' they don' 'ave to . . .' She lowered her voice and leaned over the Major to tell Aunt Irene in confidence that they only appeared when taunted by the presence of perfect goodness. 'Like flies roun' an 'oney pot,' she concluded.

'Well, *I* don't know,' said Aunt Irene. 'I think *you* must've been drinking. I can't understand a word you say.'

'Lotsa people don't,' observed the sybil complacently, 'on'y I'm a'ways right.'

It was very difficult filling the Major with the baby's orange juice, very sticky and unpleasant; and Mrs O'Connor rounded off the operation by pouring a bucket of water over him. He lay under the magnolia, gradually recovering, trembling a little, but quiet. Trickles of greenish water ran over him, looking for their own level, and he smelt faintly rotten, for the bucket had stood for some time in a corner of the garden and algae had been placidly proliferating in it.

'I can think of better ways of spending the

afternoon,' said Aunt Irene, wondering at herself, 'than sitting in the garden tending a case of terminal drunkenness.'

'Tell 'is wife to take 'im 'ome,' said Mrs O'Connor rising. 'Let the silly ole ratbag do som'ink useful.'

'The poor soul's terrified of him,' said Aunt Irene. 'And I don't honestly blame her.'

'Then she shoulda slung 'im out long since,' said Mrs O'Connor, 'give 'im the elbow.'

* * *

'What shall I cook for them?' asked Aunt Irene crossly towards the end of the week. Like many a hostess she was thoroughly resenting the guests she had invited and the trouble they would occasion her. 'I must be *mad*.' She wondered how she could punish them.'

'A cold table?' suggested Mrs Mason.

'Certainly not,' said Aunt Irene promptly. 'A simply enormous *daube* and a huge salad.' Now you've done it, she told herself. She'd had every intention of serving cold food until that wretched woman had spoken. 'Cold table' indeed! It sounded so hideously refeened.

'Whatsa dobe?' asked Victor.

'Stew,' said Aunt Irene shortly.

'You don' 'ave stew at parties,' Victor reminded her. 'You 'ave 'am and lettuce and tomaters cut in 'alf so's they look like flahs.'

106

'Oh, do be quiet,' said Aunt Irene. When she was annoyed, her face lost all animation and took on the aspect of certain puddings, sullenly lifeless and pale. Mrs Mason thought she looked like a great big baby, thoroughly spoiled. Mrs Mason became newly aware of her own aching feet and chipped fingernails and reflected that some people didn't know they were born. She took all the invitations from above the fireplace and piled them up neatly, dusting underneath. She was even tireder than usual with the effort of trying to erase from her memory the vision of that awful woman tending the Major *in extremis*. Sometimes she almost managed to persuade herself it had been a dream, but mostly she had to be content with the fantasy that people would put the Major's behaviour down to shell shock—that, at the worst, they would find him a touch eccentric.

When the telephone rang Aunt Irene jumped like a shot cat. 'You answer it,' she said to Victor.

' 'Ullo,' went Victor intimidatingly. ' 'S Lady Diana fer yer,' he said to Aunt Irene. 'Aren' we posh.'

'Who on earth was that?' enquired Diana. 'He sounds like the plumber.'

'He's the plumber,' said Aunt Irene, rather cleverly, she thought.

'Oh,' said Diana, nonplussed. She invited Aunt Irene to go to the races with her the next day. 'And then we'll come back here and have dinner,' she said, and she wouldn't take no for an answer.

'Goodness, she's bossy,' said Aunt Irene, but her depression was lifting. The mention of racing had given her an idea. 'I'm going to get dressed now,' she announced, 'and then I'll go shopping in Soho.'

Soho, thought Mrs Mason, her nose twisting. Soho, when the Home and Colonial Stores were just up the road. She noticed with satisfaction as Aunt Irene stood in the hall drawing on her gloves that her stocking seams were not precisely straight. She herself could seldom afford fully-fashioned stockings and was in the habit of drawing a line down the backs of her legs to simulate the seams without which no woman could be considered properly dressed.

*   *   *

Aunt Irene paid off her taxi in Leicester Square and went very secretively, like a woman on a dishonourable mission, down many mean streets, until she came to the shop of her friend the Maltese horse-butcher. She was very fond of horseflesh and cooked it well. Her mother's cook had always boiled it with a swatch of sweet hay and wild garlic leaves, but Aunt Irene had refined this method, using basil and a hint of cinnamon, white wine to

108

soften any coarseness, and carrots to persuade her English guests that what they were eating was quite possibly boiled beef. Horse meat had been off the ration, and no one during the war had ever questioned her about the source of the unusual amount of meat they were enjoying. It would have been the height of tactlessness and ingratitude to suggest that your hostess might be dealing on the Black Market. People had sometimes thought it was venison. No one had ever dreamed it was horse. Unthinkable. What, mused Aunt Irene, did they imagine they were eating when they tucked into platefuls of delicious Continental salami at a cold luncheon? Quite often sausage from the Balkan regions was made not only of horse, but of donkey. Sad, really, when you thought about it, she conceded. Donkeys were nice little things, but she'd never liked horses—with their barrel-like bodies stuck on those worryingly thin legs, biting at one end and kicking at the other. Thundering round race tracks with people bouncing about on top. No, the beauty of the living horse escaped Aunt Irene.

It was the Lord of the sea who was the horse-maker. He and a goddess in a rather childish competition to decide after whom the capital of Attica should be named invented, respectively, the horse and the olive in the interests of mankind. The gods (showing a bit of sense for once) judged unanimously that the olive was the more useful and beneficial and called the place Athens. And indeed, thought Aunt Irene warmly, the goddess truly deserved the honour; for the olive and its oil were among quite the best things in life. She popped into one of Soho's ubiquitous delicatessens and bought a bag of green ones.

When she got to the Maltese horse-butcher he greeted her ecstatically, wiping his hand on his apron, patting his hat and scuttling round the counter to welcome her. Most of his customers were hard-eyed restaurateurs or greyhound owners, and Aunt Irene was a pleasant change. They had a little joke—none of his beasts had ever stirred themselves to win the Derby or leap over Becher's Brook. All he offered were lazy also-rans, fresh from daisy-laden paddocks.

'About ten pounds of a really delicious cut,' said Aunt Irene. 'And will you cut it up in nice cubes—about so . . .' and she limned a little square on the air with her two forefingers.

'Is like *butter*!' exulted the knacker in a frenzy of self-congratulation.

'I *know*,' said Aunt Irene warmly and soothingly. 'I know how I can trust you.' But as he deftly cut and thrust among the piles of flesh, Aunt Irene's eyes were drawn unwittingly to the back premises where hung lean and melancholy eviscerated bodies as in Bluebeard's pantry; and she wondered for a moment what she was doing in a country where they wouldn't eat their horses but they hanged their women.

All the way back to Leicester Square, with her carrier bags full of forbidden flesh, Aunt Irene thought of the head of the horse Fallada, nailed above the gateway, speaking in pitying terms to its maiden. She took a taxi to the Ritz for a comforting tea, where as she ate tiny sandwiches and cakes she amused herself by wondering what the other ladies would say if she should leap on to one of the little tables brandishing her carrier bags, and do a sort of horse-eating dance. They would be surprised, she thought. They would find her very foreign. She felt about for half-a-crown to pay the waiter and hoped the man from the Inland Revenue wasn't watching as she emerged from the Ritz and climbed into yet another taxi.

*   *   *

Only Valentine was in the house when she returned. 'We'd better cook this now,' said Aunt Irene, 'and stick it in the frigidaire until Saturday.' The Colonel had bought the refrigerator. It was very big and not very lovely, but Aunt Irene always put a vase of flowers on it. This danced all over the top when the fridge juddered but—touch wood—hadn't fallen off the edge. It added a bit of excitement to the calm of kitchen existence.

'What is this?' asked Valentine, wiping the

111

meat free of its blood-sodden paper.

'It's horse, actually,' said Aunt Irene, faintly defiant but finding herself loath to tell Valentine a straight lie. 'Do you eat much horse at home?' she asked, in an effort to make hippophagy sound a reasonable everyday sort of thing, and realising at the same time that the negro and the horse seemed strangely incompatible. The only black person she could think of in the equine world was the one called Prince Monolulu, who was a bookie and went round race courses yelling 'I gotta horse'.

'No,' said Valentine, 'I don't think so.' A person in a horse's head came with the masked mummers who danced to the drums at Christmas time and frightened the children. Sometimes the mummers would remove one mask only to reveal another and then people died of fright. 'We eat a lot of goat,' she added. 'Curried.'

'I don't like goats,' said Aunt Irene. 'They've eaten nearly all Greece and they're stringy.' Besides she had once seen a goat behaving oddly. It had twisted its head round to its hindquarters, urinated on its nose and then stood for quite two minutes with its upper lip curled, sniffing. 'It's gone mad,' she'd said to Kyril, and Kyril had explained that gentlemen goats always did that in the breeding season. That was why they smelt that way. It hadn't made a lot of sense to Aunt

Irene at the time, and it still didn't.

'What else do you eat apart from curried goat?' she asked. 'What did you have to eat?' was her favourite question and the first she asked of returned travellers and party-goers. She would have addressed it to the risen Christ if she had been present at the time in the garden nigh to Golgotha and once she'd got over her initial surprise.

'Soup,' said Valentine. 'With potatoes and little dumplings, and salt fish and ackee . . .'

'What's ackee?' asked Aunt Irene. It sounded an improbable cuisine to bring that air of homesickness to the composed Valentine. It must just be a question of what you're used to, she thought, picturing Persephone, resolutely anorexic in the Halls of Dis until the pomegranate proved too much for her will power. Valentine ate hardly anything. Either she found English food unpalatable or she was afraid of selling her soul.

'It's fruit,' said Valentine. 'It's a bit like scrambled egg when it's cooked. You can have bacon with it.'

'Sounds delicious,' said Aunt Irene politely. She knew, better than most, that it was the height of rudeness to be seen to be turning up your nose at other people's eating habits—and anyway her family's peripatetic mode had accustomed her to eating anything as long as it was well prepared.

113

The other most important thing to remember in life was the total inadvisibility of insulting the cook. What could be more misguided and reckless? When you thought of the power wielded by the cook, it was tantamount to taunting the driver on a hairpin bend. Even for cooks without access to datum or chopped-up panthers' whiskers there were umpteen varieties of dubious fungi—to some of which there was absolutely no antidote. Once eaten, that was it. You were sick on the first day, better on the second and dead on the third. The horror. What an ass you would feel on that second day, knowing you were doomed to death by something masquerading as a mushroom and had a mere twenty-four hours to order your effects. Then there were foxgloves and the autumn crocus, not to mention the teaspoonful of putrefied catfood lurking in the fragrant depths of the curry. There were wringing out the floor-cloth into the soup and spitting in the hollandaise. There was the slow but sure method known as English cookery, which meant white flour, white sugar, too much animal fat, too much salt, murdered vegetables, bicarbonate of soda, puddings and puddings and puddings, and salad once a year as a treat for Sunday tea—lettuce, tomato, cucumber and hard-boiled egg all layered together. And tinned fruit-salad. No wonder they were such a pasty lot. And so self-righteous about it, with their boundless

114

contempt for garlic and messed-up foreign food with sauces. An exasperating people. Aunt Irene always maintained that she would eat boiled bloodhound and cassava root if they were properly cooked. The war had done a great deal to improve the health of the British—except, of course, for those who'd been killed or maimed, and Major Mason— since they'd been forced to eat less meat and sugar and more vegetables and the dark National Loaf, which was a splendid foodstuff with all the nutrients left in. Everyone had hated it.

'And the country people sell oranges and lemons in nets tied to long poles,' said Valentine, her eyes half-closed against remembered sunshine.

For some reason Aunt Irene now felt a vast and seamless Siberian melancholy creeping over her. It was to do with this child of slavers and slaves. Why should she miss the country that had ruined her people, aggressors and victims alike, and made them worse than they need have been—crueller, greedier and less happy? She could feel the tropical sun beating with careless serenity on fields and hills and valleys full of torment and grief. It was a poor thing to leave your native country, she thought, with a moment's panic, whether by choice or enforcement. As the man said, they change the sky but not their mind who rush across the sea. For a moment Aunt Irene could smell the dust of books and hear the cries of distant children playing. Her father had always insisted that his daughters should finish all their assigned reading before they were allowed to go into the garden. Anyway wanderers were trouble, either in it or causing it with their luggage and their passports and their propensity to carry disease. Strangers in town, bad news. And the indigenous population forever crying 'Go home'. They'd even said that to the Colonel, she remembered, grinning furtively: 'Go home, Yank'. It *had* annoyed him.

'Pass me the clarified butter, will you, darling,' she said. 'It's in the fridge. I'll start on this stew before it gallops away.'

Valentine meeting the cold air was back at home again. Men in tall rubber boots brought great blocks of ice in lorries and dumped them on the lawn to be broken for the ice box. She used to pick the bits of grass off them, the heat of the sun on her head and the cold of ice under her hands.

Homesickness, thought Aunt Irene, was a needless ailment when the world was full of unavoidable anguish.

Don't mention horse to *anyone*,' she said, glad that Valentine was so uncommunicative. And Valentine thought of her father sitting in the dark room at the dark gleaming table, the slatted sunlight from the blinded window tigering his sad face.

'Cheer up,' urged Aunt Irene briskly,

surprising Valentine—who wasn't feeling sad but reflective.

'People are very funny about horses,' she went on. 'English ladies fall in love with them at puberty.'

She stopped, realising that her conversation was about to take an indelicate turn. She wanted to explain that most girls progressed to preferring males of their own species—or at least their own species—by the time they grew up. If she had been talking to Kyril she would have wondered aloud why the Home Counties weren't full of little centaurs scowling from prams, trotting across lawns on their little hooves. 'Some idiot asked the centaurs to his wedding,' she said. Classical mythology while certainly indelicate, was still respectable. 'And they tried to drag the bride off by her hair, so someone stuck an antique mixing-vat up someone else's nose and the most frightful scenes of violence ensued. Blood everywhere, bones cracking, spilt wine. What a mess!' She looked round her clean tidy kitchen, at her white unblemished wine jugs, at her antique punch bowl in particular.

'No heroes,' she said decisively, 'no roaring boys will be asked to my party. Only namby-pamby cowards who make their own clothes. I do abominate heroes.' The American Colonel had once caused a furore in the Pheasantry by insisting on hitting a man who had insulted Aunt Irene. Apart from the embarrassment

117

and the chaos of spillage and breakage, Aunt Irene had been denied the chance to utter the brilliantly wounding retort which had been on the tip of her tongue. She'd regretted it ever since.

* * *

When Aunt Irene returned very late from her day at the races she felt ghastly. She tottered into Dancing Master House, her hat awry, her feet bulging out of her shoes, and squinted malevolently at Valentine who was apparent through the drawing-room door, sitting on the floor and rattling slightly.

'Telling your beads?' enquired Aunt Irene in the tone of one discovering another engaged in abominable practices.

'Throwing dice,' said Valentine, demonstrating with a gesture of her slim and beautiful wrist.

Aunt Irene, limping closer, now saw her nephew also seated on the floor clad in the type of garment the Japanese wear when intent on killing each other. He looked peaceful and pleased, so she assumed that whatever game they'd been playing he'd been winning.

'I lost a fortune today,' she said savagely, sitting down heavily and pushing her shoes off her swollen feet. 'I do think racing is the most detestable method of throwing away money ever invented. You can't even see the stupid horses except when they dash past the bit where you happen to be standing. The people are frightful, and you end up walking miles.'

'And you with your Cossack blood,' said Kyril idly throwing a six. 'Where Valentine comes from they do this all day, sitting in the sun and smoking *ganja*.'

'Very demoralising,' said Aunt Irene. 'And I *don't* have Cossack blood.'

'Not so demoralising as slinging away your money on a lot of spavined gees,' said Kyril glancing at her briefly. 'You look awful.'

His tone was mild and Aunt Irene regarded him more closely. 'What have you been up to?' she demanded. 'You've got feathers between your teeth.'

Kyril turned his amazing gaze upon her, his expression mellifluous and calm, and Aunt Irene realised with a horrible lurch of her internal organs that Kyril was intent on seducing Valentine. He was always like this when he had his eye on a new victim— reasonable and wise and quite assured of his own irresistibility. It was afterwards that he became devilish, fragmented and unsafe. Kyril wasn't like other men, in whom doubt and frustration wrought havoc. It was fulfilment that was Kyril's undoing. I should have thwarted him sometimes, thought his aunt. Now it's too late.

'And I've got indigestion,' she said

miserably, her hand on her heart. 'I don't know how Diana has the gall to ask people to eat at her house. The soup was cold and just like paper-hanger's paste. And I don't know what the second course was—it had lots of little legs. I know how it died though,' she added with dyspeptic indignation. 'It drowned in about eighteen gallons of tepid water and no one had even put in any salt. It had just gone down for the third time when she served it, and it didn't taste of *anything.*' She moaned at the waste and futility of it. 'There was red cabbage too, and that didn't taste of anything either. You'd think it would be impossible to make red cabbage not taste of anything. The lettuce was foxed, and someone had gone to enormous trouble altering the appearance of some radishes—not, in my opinion, for the better—and oh, my poor feet . . .'

There was a line in Zachariah—'I will smite every horse with astonishment and his rider with madness.' I wish he would, thought Aunt Irene, instead of just talking about it.

*　　　*　　　*

When his aunt had limped upstairs, Kyril prepared to pounce. He had never found it necessary to employ any particular technique in these circumstances. Whereas plainer men would offer champagne, flattery, meaningful glances, Kyril would merely remark in Anglo-

Saxon that he was now ready, and the object of his desire would instantly comply with his wishes.

He untied the sash of his robe and turned to Valentine. But she had gone. Somewhere someone was laughing, and for the life of him Kyril couldn't tell who it was.

Very thoughtfully he retied his sash. He was thinking that no one should ever hear of this. Not because he had been rejected, but because he didn't understand, and he had been quite sure that life could hold no surprises for him. He saw himself as one of those unusual and fortunate men who were able to understand and fully exploit the new insights that were being developed in every field of human endeavour, both scientific and philosophical. Comte, Darwin, Freud, Einstein had, each in his own way, done his bit to soothe Kyril's conscience and smooth his path towards untroubled self-indulgence. Kyril now knew that there were no gods or ghosts, only taboos and neuroses and $E = MC^2$, and very nice too. The watches of the night held no terror for Kyril, for were not all things concrete and clear, and all mysteries explained?

Take more water with it next time, my dear, he said to himself, pretending he was drunk. But he wasn't.

Under the stairs Focus was rolling about in catty paroxysms of delighted mirth. He'd never liked Aunt Irene's kitten, Kyril, who was always complaining about finding white cat hairs on his clothes and in his bread and butter; and he'd morosely witnessed Kyril's numberless conquests, comparing him with the neighbourhood's dominant tom, a scratty looking object who stalked Cheyne Row. Focus had been made a eunuch for the sake of the sweetness of the air in Dancing Master House. He was glad, because it enabled him to take a removed and measured view of affairs—human, feline and, indeed, divine.

CHAPTER FOUR

The day after the party Aunt Irene woke late. The telephone was ringing and as far as she was concerned it could go on ringing. The day of the party had started badly with an anonymous telephone call. She had had a stiff brandy, and then another, and by the time her guests arrived she had already forgotten quite a few of the preceding events of the day. She realised now with foreboding that she could remember very little of the party itself and she rose to go down and conduct the customary *post mortem*, since no matter how bad it was it was always better to know.

Valentine was busily clearing the kitchen. She said, 'Good morning.'

'I have no time for irony,' said Aunt Irene,

122

pushing a stained napkin off the rocking chair and sitting down. 'Did I fall over last night?' she asked as a bruised area made itself evident.

'I don't think so,' said Valentine. 'Some people did, but you didn't.'

'Well, some of them must have fallen on me,' concluded Aunt Irene. 'I'm hurt.'

'Mrs O'Connor's coming in soon to help,' said Valentine. 'She went straight to Mass from the party and she's gone home to change.'

'How many other people stayed the night?' asked Aunt Irene. 'I couldn't bring myself to look in any of the rooms.'

'Quite a lot,' said Valentine. 'They're all asleep.'

Aunt Irene sighed. 'Were any of them sick?' she asked. She was pleased when Mrs O'Connor arrived ready-wrapped in a blue overall, seeming capable and cheerful and not as though she'd stayed up all night.

'How did the party *go*?' asked Aunt Irene.

'Awright,' said Mrs O'Connor judiciously. 'Not bad.'

'You're just saying that,' said Aunt Irene. 'You don't want to upset me.' She could dimly visualise a little cameo of herself giving Diana a piece of her mind. 'Oh God,' she said as the scene became clearer. She squeezed her eyes tightly shut and asked for coffee.

'Mrs Mason won' be in today,' remarked

Mrs O'Connor. 'I saw 'er standin' on 'er area steps, cryin'.'

'I cannot begin to describe to you,' said Aunt Irene with profound sincerity, 'how *much* I *don't* care.' She raised her eyelids very, very carefully and looked cautiously about her, using only the bottom halves of her eyes.

' 'N' the Major's knocked off the booze,' said Mrs O'Connor. 'I wuz in the Bunch o' Grapes 'n' the barman said 'e 'adn't bin in. 'S a miracle,' she added. ' 'E seen the devil 'n' all 'is works, 'n' it give 'im such a fright 'e's gone on the wagon.'

'Nonsense,' protested Aunt Irene. 'His liver gave out, that's all. When DTs begin to look like the onset of GPI, I don't think the tissues can actually absorb any more alcohol. He'd probably explode if he took so much as a teaspoon of dry sherry.'

'A miracle,' repeated Mrs O'Connor, and she looked at Valentine.

Victor, who hadn't got his mother's stamina, wanted tea, not coffee, and was having trouble with the electric kettle. 'The frickin' fing won' work,' he declared, glaring at it with an expression at once baleful and baffled.

'You 'ave to switch the switch on, stoopid,' said his mother, doing so. 'It 'elps.'

'I'm not meself,' said Victor. 'I slep' on the floor, 'n' me bones ache. There's a lot of 'em still a-kip up there, lyin' aroun' in steamin' 'eaps.'

'Serve you right,' said Mrs O'Connor.

Whaddid you do to that man?'

'What man?' asked Victor.

'You know what one,' said his mother. 'Whaddid you do?'

'Oh, that man,' said Victor. 'I stubbed out a fag on 'is 'and.'

'Why?' asked Aunt Irene.

'Well, everyone was pushin' 'n' shovin' to get at the table, 'n' I couldn' move me arms. Then I feels this 'and on me. So I says to the bloke nex' to me "Would you please 'old me glass?", 'n' I borrows 'is fag 'n' I stubs it out on this 'and, 'n' there's this 'orrible moan from three bodies away.'

'That's a bit ruthless,' said Aunt Irene, not over-pleased to hear of her guests being assaulted in this fashion.

'Filfy ole queen,' said Victor.

'I fort 'e left pretty damn quick,' said Mrs O'Connor to her child. 'Then I saw you laughin'.'

'I hope it wasn't anybody important,' said Aunt Irene.

''E didn' *look* important,' said Mrs O'Connor.

'Wuz some ole geezer what wanted a warm lovin' relationship wiv a nasty rough workin'-class bloke,' said Victor. 'I 'eard 'im earlier. Sauce.'

'Oh God,' said Aunt Irene, her hands to her eyes.

'I say,' said Kyril, entering and speaking

125

affectedly. There were days when Kyril chose to impersonate an invert—and very annoying he could be. 'You *did* go for Diana, didn't you.'

'Did I?' said Aunt Irene nervously.

'You said . . .' began Kyril.

'I don't want to know,' said Aunt Irene, her hands now to her ears. 'I do not wish to know anything about it.'

'You keep telling me,' insisted Kyril, 'not to offend her in any way, and then you—'

'Don't,' implored Aunt Irene.

After a while she asked, 'Might she have thought I was just joking? Teasing her?'

'No,' said Kyril.

Aunt Irene braced herself. 'All right,' she said resignedly. 'What did I say?'

Kyril settled down in a chair. 'Well,' he began. 'It started when she saw Valentine, and she said "Who's that?", rather as though a lizard had sneaked out from under the carpet, and you bridled a bit and said she was a friend of your sister's . . .'

'What an odd way of expressing myself,' interrupted Aunt Irene. 'Go on.'

'And she said soothingly that Valentine had very fine lines. And you weren't soothed and said she wasn't a horse, for goodness' sake, and Diana got annoyed and said she wasn't suggesting she was—she was merely speculating that Valentine must have white aristocratic blood somewhere and that one of her ancestors was probably some remittance

126

man of good family. And you said that in your opinion the English upper classes mostly resembled rabbits, or possibly dogs, and the best-looking person with the most noble features you'd ever seen was fooling about with a basketful of snakes in the Place Djemaa el F'na in Marrakesh, and she told you not to be silly, and then you went on about the beauty of chaps who hide in holes along the Khyber Pass and the ineffable grace of the Xhosa, and she said she thought you'd gone mad, and you said mad you might be but at least people could eat the food in your house.'

'Did I say that?' said Aunt Irene, awed. 'I must have been paralytically plastered.'

'You wuz a bit far gone,' said Mrs O'Connor, 'but you wuz awright. On yer feet.'

'Did she leave then?' asked Aunt Irene.

'Not 'er,' said Mrs O'Connor. 'She 'adn't 'ad 'er dinner.'

'She couldn't find Cassandra,' said Kyril, 'and she wouldn't go without her.'

'I was talking to Cassandra,' said Valentine, 'under the little tree in the front garden.'

Kyril looked up. He'd spent the entire evening searching for Valentine. He'd circled that magnolia at least a dozen times. He stared at her.

'The best bit was the dancin',' said Mrs O'Connor. 'We done the Conga all roun' the 'ouses till the neighbours got stroppy.'

Aunt Irene sat bolt upright. 'Dancing!' she

127

said. 'He was there. He was dancing, the tax man. I saw him.'

'Oh, rubbish,' said Kyril.

'I tell you I saw him,' said Aunt Irene. '*He* was dancing all by himself.'

'That was Mr Sirocco,' said Kyril. 'He was dancing all by himself.'

'I know the difference between the tax man and little Mr Sirocco,' said Aunt Irene. 'I'm not quite mad.'

'No,' allowed Kyril, 'but you were unusually tight.'

It was forbidden to dance alone to a tune inaudible to others. Valentine knew that.

'You were telling everyone the story of the dancing master,' said Kyril. 'It was probably weighing on your mind.'

'Are you sure?' asked Aunt Irene. 'I have no recollection of telling anyone anything.'

All Religious love stories. Valentine turned round from the sink. 'I didn't hear it,' she said. 'I didn't know there was a story.'

'It's a ghost story,' said Kyril, showing his teeth and calling to mind not the ghosts of England but the shades and demons of great northern forests, trolls and blood-suckers and unspeakable ogres.

'We have ghosts,' said Valentine, unperturbed. 'Big ones and little ones. And the undead—they don't really matter.'

'Well, no, I suppose they don't,' said Aunt Irene, disconcerted.

128

'But they make good stories,' said Valentine. 'Sometimes it's better when things aren't true.'

'I'll tell you then,' said Aunt Irene. 'I'm not really strong enough to do anything today but sit around and tell stories. Once upon a time . . .' she commenced.

'No, no,' said Kyril, as only a close relation can. 'That isn't the way to begin. You have to start with the house.'

'*I'm* telling this story,' said Aunt Irene. But Kyril was right.

'We believe,' she resumed, 'that the original house was built in the reign of Henry the Hateful in the grounds of a manor that fronted on the river. It was a very small house designed for a very small person—you can see the outline of one of the original doors at the bottom of the staircase. It was the sort of exquisite box a man might build for his mistress, but *this* house was built for a man.'

' 'S why it's called Dancin' Master 'Ouse,' said Mrs O'Connor. She laughed in a ribald way.

'He was a dancing master,' explained Aunt Irene glaring rather at Mrs O'Connor. It was quite impossible—recounting tales in the presence of people who knew them already. She wondered how Taliesin, Demodocus and all the other storytellers had coped.

'There was tremendous competition for the services of the best Italian masters because the Tudor *nouveaux riches* were the most frightful clod-hopping thugs,' she went on. 'The house was probably built as a bribe to secure him exclusively for the family.

'Now the family was odd. It consisted of a spice merchant, his wife, his sister-in-law and her daughters, and they had umpteen cooks and scullions and abigails and ostlers and grooms and stable boys . . .' She stopped, wondering irritatedly why she'd developed this compulsion to go on and on about horses and related topics. 'Anyway, at some point there was a dreadful scandal. Most of the evidence was lost in the Great Fire, but a few scraps of documents survived until the beginning of the war—including a letter quoting a servant girl who "heard a great stirre upon the bed with many other fowle circumstances".'

'Cor,' interjected Victor.

'Nobody knows any longer who precisely was involved with whom, or what happened. Only one day somebody scavenging in the mud found the dancing master floating face down, his poor little dancing shoes all wet. The family sank back into obscurity, the manor house fell down, and a ship's chandler used the little house to store things in—nautical things. It stayed standing all the time while the city grew, though by the eighteenth century hardly any of the original structure remained. Then, during the Regency, some spec builder bought it with the surrounding land and built this row of houses, which is more or less what you see today.' She added, untruthfully, that when the mists were thick on the river and the tug boats gloomily hooted you could sometimes hear the sound of the tap-tap-tapping of little leather-soled shoes.

'Izzat true?' demanded Victor, who made a child's tiresome distinction between fact and fantasy.

'What is truth?' enquired Aunt Irene, who really was quite unclear about it.

'Cassandra had a row with some people,' said Kyril.

'*Cassandra?*' said Aunt Irene incredulously. Cassandra was a peaceful and pusillanimous girl. 'What on earth about?'

'Religion,' said Kyril. 'Celibacy. I was rather relieved. I hope she takes it up. She's been eyeing me like a hungry hyena for months.'

'You're so *conceited*,' said his aunt fondly. 'What did she say?'

'Well, someone said the monastic life was selfish. And she said yes, wasn't it marvellous how amazingly unselfish married people were—always giving things to beggars and tearing their coats in half and generally behaving in an altruistic and Christ-like fashion. She was being ironical, you understand.'

'I understand,' said Aunt Irene, who didn't. Cassandra had never been ironical before.

'Then someone said religion was responsible for a vast amount of human

131

unhappiness, and she said that in her experience it was sex that made people most unhappy, and she'd never met a girl who was buying six bottles of aspirins because God had got her into trouble and run away; and someone said "What about the B. V. M. ?" and she gave them a very old-fashioned look, and then she said she'd never come across a girl teetering on a window sill because God had left her for the blonde next door. And then she said God had never blacked anyone's eye for refusing his favours. She went on like that for quite a bit.'

'Good heavens,' said Aunt Irene. 'Was she drunk?'

'No,' said Kyril, shaking his head and shrugging his shoulders.

'How very peculiar,' said Aunt Irene. And she thought of the child Jesus discoursing to the Elders while his parents flew around distractedly searching for him—'You go and look in the Brook Cedron while I dash up to the Street called Straight.' Or was that Damascus? Anyway, thought Aunt Irene, if she'd been Mary and Joseph she'd have shaken him till his teeth rattled. God or no God.

'Valentine was a splendid success,' said Kyril. 'People kept propositioning her.'

Valentine was used to this. When they heard she was to be a nun, wizened dwarfs, senile deliquescent lechers, gross and hideous

132

husbands all began to swagger and to indicate that this was mere virginal foolishness and if she would but just taste of the joys of life—this meant *them*—she would abandon her plan and take up that position for which she was most suited, i.e. flat on her back and grateful for it. They said the same sort of thing to the prettier lesbians.

'Little Mr Sirocco asked her to marry him,' Kyril disclosed.

'To dance with him,' corrected Valentine. 'But I don't dance.'

'I've seen you dancing,' said Kyril. 'You dance in the morning, early.'

'When are you ever up in the morning early?' snapped Aunt Irene, oddly perturbed by his words.

'When I haven't been to bed all night,' said Kyril reasonably. 'When I coincide with the milk. Besides,' he added, 'she must have been dancing, because Diana said they all had such a marvellous sense of rhythm.' He sighed with satisfaction. 'It makes life almost worth while when people are so perfectly predictable. There's a beautiful mathematical certainty about Diana's thought processes. Knowing precisely what she's going to say next gives one a sense of omnipotence—I don't believe I should be happy if I couldn't listen to Diana sometimes.'

Aunt Irene frowned. This was Kyril at his worst—manipulative and inhuman. Of course

Diana was a pain in the neck, but she was a *person*, not a mechanical toy to amuse Kyril. It was all right, reasoned Aunt Irene—quite clearly, considering the state of her hangover—to be annoyed by stupidity and insensitivity, but it was far from all right to be coldly delighted by it.

Mrs O'Connor wondered whether Kyril had seen Valentine dancing in the air. You could never tell with Kyril. He probably wouldn't say if he didn't think he could make some sort of trouble by doing so. She looked at him, and she thought he was bad. When he left for work she was glad, because the room felt lighter and brighter. She was herself an extremely sinful woman and the despair of her confessor, but she considered herself not to be evil, and as the word went through her mind she crossed herself.

Aunt Irene, noting this pious gesture, felt rather like someone whose domestic hygiene has been called into question. She was offended, annoyed; yet, like a housewife who has neglected to clean behind the sofa, she knew there was some justice in Mrs O'Connor's tacit remark. She wished again she had been harder on Kyril, but she had always found it difficult to refuse anything to a beauty. To Aunt Irene beauty demanded tribute, and in consequence Kyril resembled a dangerous baby to whom his own desires were of paramount importance and any denial of his wishes manifest of a cosmic outrage. Well, there was nothing she could do about it now, short of dismantling him entirely and starting again, and she sighed. Two worried middle-aged women, who only the night before had been very merry, began to clean up after the party, each troubled by a sense of encroaching shadow.

*   *   *

Focus found the atmosphere lowering and asked to be let out of the front door.

'Well, be careful,' warned Aunt Irene. 'Some awful person might make you into a muff. Don't leave the garden.'

Normally Focus wouldn't have dreamed of leaving the garden. He would sit under the magnolia daring its blossom to compete with his beauty, and watching the birds, but he was no different from anyone else when it came to being ordered about. He didn't like it.

As soon as Aunt Irene closed the door Focus stepped on to the pavement and gazed round warily. He was perfectly sensible of the dangers inherent in being so attractive, and was taking no risks. Aunt Irene had a very sinister sepia-tinted photograph of one of her relations on a snowy railway station wearing a hat which looked to Focus as though it might well be related to him.

There was no one in the street, so he went

135

for a little walk towards the church waving his tail, and there, sitting on a garden wall was that rat. Major Mason saw it too, only he didn't believe it. He was out for a constitutional, because he was determined to become very healthy now that he had given up drinking, and this rat vision struck him as most unfair. He knew it must be a hallucination because that dopey-looking cat was taking no notice of it at all. Poor Major Mason couldn't know that Focus was merely going to some lengths to maintain his dignity, having been had before.

Major and cat passed each other looking steadily ahead while the rat smirked. Focus went home and tapped on the dining-room window, and the Major went down to the river to breathe in some refreshing effluent.

*   *   *

' 'Oo was Ganymede?' asked Mrs O'Connor after a while.

'A sort of waiter,' said Aunt Irene. 'Why?'

'Well,' said Mrs O'Connor, 'Valentine was dolin' out the dinner 'n' this old man says, "Ah, Phoebe . . ."'

'Hebe,' corrected Aunt Irene, assuming she was in the right myth.

'. . . 'n' 'e says "But where's Ganymede?" I fink 'e wuz lookin' for Kyril.'

'I can't think why,' said Aunt Irene. Kyril had never helped anyone to anything in all his

136

life. It must be another example of that fantasy wish-fulfilment one heard so much about. Zeus had paid in horses for Ganymede. Horses, horses, mused Aunt Irene. *Damn* horses. 'If I didn't think it would kill me,' she said, 'I'd have a brandy.'

' 'S not a bad idea,' said Mrs O'Connor. ' 'S long as you put a bit o' milk 'n' a bit o' melted bacon fat in it.'

'Ow, urgh, don't,' said Aunt Irene, clutching her mouth.

' 'S true,' said Mrs O'Connor. 'Settles the stummick.'

Half an hour later Aunt Irene, who had amended Mrs O'Connor's prescription to the extent of leaving out the bacon fat, was indeed feeling better. As they gave the remains of the horse stew to Focus, they both giggled.

'Gee up,' remarked Mrs O'Connor.

'How did you know?' asked Aunt Irene.

'Me mum was a gypsy,' explained Mrs O'Connor. 'I know 'orse flesh. D'you see 'em all eatin' it up? Laugh? I fort m' knickers 'd never dry.'

'I feel pale,' said Aunt Irene. 'Valentine makes me feel pale. She makes everyone look so unhealthy and maggot-like.' She poured herself another brandy and added, 'Behold, a pale horse, and his name that sat on him was Death, and Hell followed with him.'

Which was when the man next door arrived with the dreadful news.

137

CHAPTER FIVE

Aunt Irene was still in a state of shock when Kyril came home. She met him on the doorstep like any common woman, fat and portentous with news, not waiting until they were properly enclosed between walls to tell him the tidings.

'Little Mr Sirocco's dead,' she said, and Kyril said, 'Hooray.'

'No, no,' said Aunt Irene, 'you don't understand. He's *really* dead.'

'Then *really* hooray,' said Kyril, and at these terrible words just for a moment Aunt Irene felt that she didn't love Kyril or find him amusing at all.

*　　　*　　　*

'He hanged himself,' said Aunt Irene of little Mr Sirocco, for the eighteenth time. 'He tied all his ties together and hanged himself from the curtain rail, and the tie round his neck was his old school tie. He was so *determined*.' She was amazed at that determination. Little Mr Sirocco had been tentative, nebulous and unsure. It was uncharacteristic of him to die with such conviction.

'Why did no one see him from the street?' she wondered aloud. 'They can't have taken him for the curtains.' She remembered unwillingly that the hanged, as they die, dance in the air.

* * *

When she had discussed the matter to dust with the people present she telephoned Diana and started again.

Diana was very cool.

'I'm sorry,' said Aunt Irene. 'I didn't mean to scream at you last night.'

'I don't mind that. I'm quite used to that,' said Diana insultingly. 'No, what I'm really cross about is that wretched girl you have staying with you. She's had the most terrible influence on Cassandra. Cassandra says she's going to become a nun.' Her tone would have led anyone overhearing who didn't speak the language to suppose that 'nun' was the dirtiest word in the lexicon.

'Cassandra's a silly girl,' said Aunt Irene, not thinking. 'You haven't heard the dreadful news.'

But Diana wasn't interested in the dreadful news. She concluded the conversation even more coolly than she'd begun it.

'Oh hell,' said Aunt Irene. 'Valentine, what have you done? Cassandra's going to take the veil and she isn't even a Catholic.'

'She'd make a good nun,' said Valentine.

'How can you possibly know that?' asked

Aunt Irene, momentarily diverted from her current obsession.

'She's a bit like me,' said Valentine.

Aunt Irene wondered whether she should write to her sister informing her of the death next door to Dancing Master House. For an enclosed nun, Reverend Mother had an extraordinary and inconvenient facility for keeping up to date with events. It seemed that nothing escaped her notice, and Aunt Irene felt it would be better to get in first with her own version. Perhaps she could mention that she was sending along a brand-new convert to swell the diminishing ranks of sisters—though she'd have to be very careful. Claiming credit on the one hand for Cassandra's conversion and on the other denying all responsibility would require skilful manoeuvring. Diana would never forgive her if she suspected she was encouraging Cassandra, who at this very moment was skipping down the street on her way to instruction with the curate. The PP wasn't strong enough to take on any additional duties.

*　　　*　　　*

Cassandra called at Dancing Master House when her lesson was over. She looked even younger than usual—newly washed and lamb-like, yet curiously stubborn.

'Do we know our penny catechism yet?'

140

asked Kyril.

Cassandra looked at him without love.

'What do we make of the Infallibility of the Pope?' enquired Kyril, following this with the Real Presence, the Immaculate Conception, the Devotion of the Sacred Heart, and the Inquisition.

As far as anyone could gather, since she didn't say very much, Cassandra took exception to none of them.

'The curate is a fortunate fellow,' said Kyril. 'You must make his task very simple.'

'*I'm* very simple,' said Cassandra, showing some of that new aggression that had so startled the party guests.

'No, no,' soothed Aunt Irene, 'not simple.'

'Simple,' insisted Cassandra, looking faintly dangerous. So they left it at that.

*   *   *

Reverend Mother yet again opened the drawer of her desk, prepared to look hopelessly within at the gleaming, maddening symbol of the power of God.

But wait. What was this? She looked closer. The apple was dimmer, its sheen diminished. And surely that was a flaw on its scarlet skin. Oh joy. Soon, thought Reverend Mother, it would be as wrinkled as the face of the oldest nun, and Valentine could come back and warm their hearts.

141

She was so pleased she summoned the convent chaplain and told him, and he was pleased too. He hadn't been long at the convent and was getting very tired through simultaneously developing, and attempting to suppress, a detestation of women in general and nuns in particular. He badly missed his parish in Liverpool 8—and his budgerigars, which he hadn't been able to bring with him because there were so many of them they needed an aviary. He'd been ill, you see, and his superiors thought it would be a good idea to put him in a convent in Wales, but *he* thought it was a lousy idea and longed for the fog of the Mersey. Valentine reminded him of some of his parishioners. Everything would be much brighter when Valentine came back.

*   *   *

Victor came round to clear out little Mr Sirocco's effects.

'His family may want his things,' suggested Aunt Irene.

'Nah,' said Mrs O'Connor. 'They'd just upset 'em.'

'I rather think they may be more upset if they don't get his watch and cufflinks and little oddments like that,' insisted Aunt Irene—quite sternly for her—perhaps because her righteous sister, Berthe, hadn't yet left her mind.

'Oh well, o' *course*,' conceded the O'Connors largely, 'we'll give 'em those.'

'Oh yes,' said Aunt Irene.

'First fing I'll do termorrer,' said Mrs O'Connor, 'is wash them curtains. The Nottin'ham lace.'

This change of subject wasn't entirely successful, causing Aunt Irene to reflect on the inadvisability of hanging stolen goods at your windows for the world to consider. She thought for a moment that life might be simpler if she mended her ways, paid her taxes, bought things through legitimate outlets and didn't give people horses to eat.

The ringing of the telephone dispelled this defeatism. She knew before she reached it that on the end of the line would be the silent communicant; and suddenly, like volatile chemicals, the shock and depression and worry that had been so troubling her merged and ignited in a great blaze of vengeful rage. 'I'll get him,' she vowed aloud. She addressed Mrs O'Connor. 'Bring Jimmy round tonight,' she commanded, 'and we'll work out a battle plan, because truly I will not go on being harrassed and haunted by that horribly inferior little person.' Aunt Irene's selective form of snobbery added fuel to the flames.

'That's it, gel.' (All the O'Connors pronounced their final *l*'s as *w*'s, but there isn't any way of indicating this in print.)

Mrs O'Connor grinned and bristled with

143

approval, flexing her muscles and practising belligerent little sideways prancing steps, jabbing at the air and squinting. And indeed Aunt Irene, too, felt an unwomanly desire to inflict actual physical damage on the tax man.

'I'm sure he's out there every night,' she said. 'People have seen him and I can sense him.'

* * *

Kyril returned, humming dreamily, his keys dangling from a languid finger.

'Where have you been?' demanded Aunt Irene, as God had once asked of Satan—who'd replied that he'd been going to and fro about the world and walking up and down in it.

Kyril merely said he'd been out. 'I met Valentine,' he added, glancing sideways and upwards at his aunt through narrowed eyes. 'She was down by the river watching the flow of contraceptives to the sea.'

'I don' like 'er,' announced Victor.

''Oo cares 'oo you like?' said his mother, you silly fing.'

'Why didn't she come back with you?' demanded Aunt Irene.

'She went to church,' said Kyril. 'Perhaps she has things to confess.'

Aunt Irene and Mrs O'Connor spoke simultaneously. Aunt Irene snapped, 'Yes, and perhaps she hasn't'; and Mrs O'Connor said, very decisively, 'Not 'er.'

Now Kyril and Victor spoke together. Kyril said 'How do you know?', and Victor said ''Ow d'yer know?' They both sounded cross, and Kyril also sounded peeved. His voice had taken on a waspish edge.

Mother and aunt gazed with scorn and anxiety at these invincibly ignorant young males. 'If you can't see that,' said Aunt Irene, 'you can't see anything.' And Mrs O'Connor said 'Soppy great lollop', including Kyril in the observation.

'She's a woman, isn't she?' asked Kyril, goaded by sudden doubt out of his habitual self-satisfaction.

'Ooh,' cried Aunt Irene on a note of exasperated despair. 'Sometimes I *know* you don't understand *anything*. You don't understand about people, and you don't understand about God.'

'*God*,' said Kyril, laughing lightly.

Aunt Irene shivered. It had occurred to her the other day in church that possibly it was only the good who were *able* to believe in God—that the wicked, being hideously narcissistic, could see only themselves reflected in whatever they looked upon; could believe only in their own desires and inadequacies, were quite incapable of seeing the truth of a different person or deity.

Like people who took sugar in their tea, or people cross-eyed and dribbling with lust. Such

145

people when told that other people preferred their tea unsweetened, or liked to sleep alone, simply did not believe it—were quite *unable* to believe it.

The only answer was for these people to practise virtue, no matter what they felt like. To do good things until it became clear to them that good things could be done. And perhaps in the end the snake scales would fall from their eyes, and they would be able to see the limpidity of God, and after a while it would cease to offend them. Of course the same thing applied to the virtuous. The virtuous were unable to see the attractions of lying dead drunk in the gutter, or tearing frenziedly from bed to bed, or telling lies or pushing old ladies out of railway trains. If the virtuous should try doing these things in order not to set themselves apart from other people they would lay themselves open to the charge of hypocrisy. But then that applied to the wicked too. Perhaps it didn't matter. Perhaps there were worse things than hypocrisy.

'Kyril,' she said, 'I wish you'd take up good works. Nothing too strenuous. Just a bit of visiting the sick, or burying the dead. The odd cardinal work of mercy—'

Kyril merely shot her a look. He didn't even laugh. He'd never heard anything so fatuous in all his days.

*   *   *

146

Reverend Mother wrote to Aunt Irene, heading her letter 'The Feast of St Silverius'. She said she thought Valentine should return to the Mother House quite soon, but gave no reasons.

Aunt Irene was desolated. When Valentine left it would be as though the fire had gone out, the sun gone in. She would take away not only her own warmth and colour, but the warmth and colour from everything about her. A thief, thought Aunt Irene sadly. Just like the O'Connors.

*   *   *

Mrs Mason got up early. She walked on the edges of her feet in an effort not to wake the Major, and scarcely breathed. In the kitchenette—a lowering, lightless strip partitioned off from the living room by sheets of plywood and offering a perspective on to the area coal hole—she tried to strike a match very quietly to light the gas ring. There was no oven, and everything the Masons ate was either boiled or fried or cold or raw. Even the gas made a shocking noise, hissing at her.

She hissed back at it admonitorily. 'You'll wake the Major,' she cried soundlessly, 'you'll wake the Major.'

She closed her eyes as she turned on the tap very slowly and held the kettle close to it. Her

147

face was taut with strain, and her teeth ground together. The lino under the sink was torn, and the Major was wont to trip over it. There was no reason in the world for the Major ever to go into the kitchenette; but he did, and every time he tripped over the lino. Then he'd swear, and yell, and his wife's eyes would widen with terror and she'd call him 'dear' and offer to make him a cup of tea if only he'd come and sit down and let her look after him. Then he'd call her evil names and let her see how he despised her craven twittering.

Really, she should have murdered him, but she lacked the initiative. Her plan now was to get dressed, give him his breakfast and leave immediately for work. His days were quite empty now that he no longer drank, and he didn't like her going out. When she went shopping he went with her and prevented her from buying necessities, saying he wasn't made of money, and then when there was no tea in the place, or milk or matches, he'd shout. She wished and wished that he'd take up drink again, spend his days in the Bunch of Grapes and his nights in a drunken stupor. He was awful drunk, but he was worse sober.

She crept into the bedroom like a tall, bowed mouse and slid her clothes silently off the chair where they lay. Today she would wear the sea-green dress, and perhaps her husband would think her pretty and not abuse her. She dressed in the sitting-room and then went to boil his egg. It was torture boiling the Major's egg for it had to be just right—not too hard or too soft or too hot or too cold, and certainly not cracked. Oh lord, if his egg was cracked . . . Mrs Mason whimpered. The tray laid—the cutlery on a napkin, so that it wouldn't rattle—she went to wake him.

He was up and dressed.

'Dear,' she said, 'I was just coming to wake you.'

'You woke me already,' he said, 'crashing round like a bull elephant.'

'Oh, I am sorry,' she said. 'Silly me.' She was breathlessly relieved to find him in a good mood and went to the lavatory since it was now safe to pull the chain.

'I must run,' she said. 'I'm going to do the shopping on the way.'

'I'll come with you,' said her husband benevolently, downing the last of his egg.

*   *   *

There was a smell of hot pavement as they ascended the area steps, and the light hurt Mrs Mason's eyes. Everything in the flat had either darkened or faded to the same dull, mournful beige, and unconfined daylight came as something of a surprise. She hoped her make-up would be adequate to this pitiless glare and surreptitiously touched the corners of her nose where powder tended to gather and cake.

On the Kings Road she contrived to see her reflection in the shop windows and was pleased with the sea-green frock—it was cut with that flair and style that seemed to have left the country with the Duchess of Windsor, never to return. She straightened her shoulders and held her head up feeling young and smart—what the Major used to call 'a fine filly'.

They stopped at the newsagents to buy a morning paper for the Major, and Mrs Mason stood, idly and elegantly, her head thoughtfully tilted, as he made his transaction.

Lifting her head, she was surprised to find herself staring straight into the face of a furious stranger, and she backed away into a rack of magazines. It was odd. The woman was certainly a total stranger, and equally certainly it was Mrs Mason with whom she was so angry. For a tiny horrified moment Mrs Mason thought she knew how Valentine must feel, loathed on sight for something you couldn't help. She looked round for support. The woman was whispering agitatedly to her companion, another woman who, as she got the gist of the whispers, looked as angry as her friend. Together they glared at her, their mouths set with hostility, their eyes narrowed.

Mrs Mason began to sweat with nerves. The green frock seemed suddenly constricting and the shop airless. She sidled towards the Major.

The woman was now talking quite loudly

and the other customers were beginning to turn and stare.

'I tell you it's mine,' the woman was saying. 'My aunt gave me those clip buttons specially and I sewed them on myself. I'd know it anywhere.'

Mrs Mason's hands flew to her throat. Mrs O'Connor, that terrible thief! She thought she was going to faint.

'Good morning, Mrs Mason,' said a voice. 'I like your blue frock.' Valentine was standing between her and the women.

'It's green,' began Mrs Mason frailly, looking down at herself. But it wasn't. It was, in this light, undeniably blue, and the material was coarser than she remembered, the thread in the centre seam clumsily drawn.

'Turquoise,' she said, feeling suddenly stronger. 'Such a deceptive shade, especially in this shot material. Sometimes blue, sometimes green—like a zircon.'

'Like the sea,' said Valentine.

Mrs Mason now realised who she was talking to—in public—and said goodbye very coldly. She went out with the Major, who, deaf to these female entanglements, was flipping through the day's fixtures as he walked.

The woman bereft of the green dress was staring open-mouthed and blushing slightly. 'I could've sworn . . .' she said. 'I couldn't have been mistaken.'

'You never know,' said her friend, who was

clearly easily influenced. 'Not with that shade of turquoise.'

*   *   *

Little Mr Sirocco's family called briefly to thank Aunt Irene for being good to him. As they left, they said they simply couldn't believe he was dead.

'I don't know why,' said Kyril, the front door barely closed behind them. 'Most people are. When you think how many bodies have been inserted in Mother Earth, it's a sort of miracle she hasn't sagged with the strain and plummeted out of space.'

'I know de feelin',' said Mrs O'Connor unexpectedly, and laughed. 'God rest 'is soul,' she added in a more respectable voice.

'The man next door said the room was full of pigeon feathers when they found him,' said Kyril.

'Oh dear, perhaps he was so lonely he flung open the window and asked the birds in,' suggested Aunt Irene.

'He couldn't have done,' said Kyril. 'He was phobic about birds. It was one of his things. He really was very mixed up.'

'So he was,' said Aunt Irene, remembering. 'Funny about birds, I mean. But surely that wouldn't make him hang himself? Just think. Now I don't like snakes a bit, but if I found myself in a room full of them, all slithering about and hissing, I might climb on the table or jump out of the window, but I wouldn't calmly sit there tying things together to hang myself with. Then of course, if it was birds, you'd only get nearer to them if you climbed on the table or jumped out of the window—if you follow me. I mean, that's where they are. Unless they happen to be walking at the time—they do a lot of that recently. But then all he had to do was rush out of the room. I don't understand. He didn't mind eating eggs,' she added suddenly.

'Bet it was the fevvers what got 'im,' said Mrs O'Connor. 'I 'ad an auntie like that once. Jus' the sight of a fevver boa or a Pearlie's 'at 'n' she'd go off in screamin' 'ysterics.'

'Well, I think it's awful,' said Aunt Irene, her face as pale as gooseberry fool. 'I feel dreadful. If only he'd come to me . . .'

'You couldn't have done anything,' said Kyril authoritatively (he was an expert on suicide). 'He was determined to succeed at his first attempt.'

'But why?' implored Aunt Irene. '*Why?*' She felt responsible, which was one of the few penalties her degree of self-centredness would necessarily incur.

'It was nothing to do with you or anyone else,' explained Kyril, who was far more solipsistic than his aunt but differently constituted: he had no feelings of responsibility at all. 'People who lay violent
153

hands on themselves are always, deep down, determined to die. Even those whose attempts are interpreted as a "cry for help" . . .' here Kyril's Attic mouth folded in a sneer '. . . mean to die. Even those who stick their head in the gas oven five minutes before their wife is due to arrive really hope she won't. It just makes them feel less guilty.'

Aunt Irene supposed that Kyril should know. An extraordinary number of his friends had killed themselves or attempted to do so, reappearing in the pub with their complexions permanently encarmined by carbon monoxide, their wrists bandaged, their stomachs pumped. Some of them, in the end, had taken a room in a high hotel and jumped out of the topmost window, enraging the local hotel managers, who had enough trouble trying to decide who were legitimately married, or able to pay the bill, without having to debate with themselves whether or not a potential guest had leanings towards *felo de se*.

An inconvenient and unwelcome sensation of cosmic pity rose in Aunt Irene. She longed to fling open the doors of Dancing Master House to all those poor creatures who loved themselves so little that they destroyed themselves. She felt for a moment that she could love them enough to make up for all their sorrows and deprivations, and for the very first time she thought she understood her sister's motives in devoting her life to the

154

contemplation of God. If, reasoned Aunt Irene, you could lean against God as against a wall, then, your retreat covered, you could radiate good will and calm secure affection with no trouble at all.

'I'm going to church,' she said.

* * *

As she walked, she wondered what Valentine thought about the death of Mr Sirocco. She'd said nothing. Probably, thought Aunt Irene, she shared Berthe's view. Berthe, sounding mildly surprised at finding her sister weeping on the untimely death of a friend, had said, 'But death is nothing, nothing . . .'

Which could mean anything, thought Aunt Irene. It could mean you had total faith, or no faith at all, and it wasn't much help to the ordinary mortal.

It was good for her peace of mind that she hadn't overheard Kyril telling Valentine it was probably her fault Mr Sirocco had died— grieving over her rejection of him, because Valentine had replied that it was Kyril whom Mr Sirocco had loved and Kyril had gone a very horrible unhealthy colour and had had to sit down. His own reaction had surprised him and made him rather thoughtful; for, in the ordinary way, he wouldn't have cared if every nut in Chelsea had hanged himself. In response, the perverse and convoluted

155

processes of his psyche had led him to behave in a more precious and effeminate manner than was entirely natural to him, and he occasionally minced or flounced.

*   *   *

'It's going to rain,' Cassandra told her grandmother.

'Nonsense,' replied Diana. 'It's a perfectly lovely day.' She wished at once that she hadn't spoken like this, for she had planned to have a wise and reasonable discussion with her granddaughter—this was how she put it to herself. In truth, of course, she meant to tell Cassandra what to do in no uncertain terms, though in as calm a voice as she could manage.

'Well, you may be right,' she said grudgingly, gazing out at the flawless sky, thinking that her daughter's child was indubitably half-witted, and blaming her son-in-law whose dreamy attitude had destroyed his wife and himself in a motoring accident on a clear road.

'Your mother expected you to marry,' she began, although she had no way of knowing this, since Cassandra's mother had died when she was two and had never expressed any views on the subject.

Cassandra said nothing. She stood by the grand piano in the first-floor drawing-room and looked longingly at the door, not realising how annoying this was.

'Are you listening to me, Cassandra?' demanded Diana.

'Yes,' said Cassandra reluctantly, untruthfully and still half-looking at the door.

'Sit down,' said Diana. 'Sit in that chair and look at *me*.'

Very slowly Cassandra obeyed her. She bore the appearance, thought her grandmother, of a cocker spaniel about to turn nasty; and she remembered that those charming, affectionate, over-bred creatures could turn very nasty indeed—foaming, biting and flinging themselves about in fits, their ears wildly flapping.

'Now, I want you to be sensible,' she said, 'and listen to me.'

Cassandra sat down, still wearing that lowering ominous dog-like expression and saying nothing.

This exasperated Diana even further, and her voice rose. Shuddering with Protestant horror and disgust, she disclosed that it was known that under every convent lay a tunnelled passage to the nearest monastery and that the younger nuns spent a great deal of time in hideous agony giving birth to illegitimate monklings who were then summarily strangled and flung into bottomless *oubliettes*.

Cassandra, whose expression had been lightening throughout this account, laughed. She had feared that her grandmother would

157

appeal to sentiment and duty, would speak of her advancing age (though if she'd thought about it for a moment she'd have realised Diana would never do *that*), would beg Cassandra to stay and warm her grandmother's declining years. It would have been difficult to resist such an approach, since her intention to enter the convent indicated that she wished to be good, and the good didn't thwart the wishes of tearful old ladies. Cassandra had worried greatly over this dilemma and now felt grateful to her grandmother for not imposing it upon her. She felt no compunction at all in leaving the vindictive and foul-mouthed person who was clearly in the best of health or could not have given vent to such passionate virulence.

Diana, seeing that she had somehow handled the thing wrongly, told Cassandra to go away, for the sight of her made her ill.

*   *   *

It rained that afternoon—a short brutal shower that indiscriminately beat the roses and flooded the sewers.

'Drops as big as tea cups,' complained Aunt Irene, wringing out the skirt of her frock as she stood in the hallway. She glared irately through the open front door at the scruffy rivulets scurrying down the gutter. 'I was half way home when it started—and, of course, not a taxi in sight. Look at that foul rain washing all the colour out of the antirrhinums.' She stared forbiddingly at Valentine and Mrs O'Connor. 'I know someone's going to say we needed it,' she said, 'and I won't have it, so don't.'

The magnolia clapped its leaves with a melancholy macintosh sound as Aunt Irene closed the door on it.

'There's wild pigs livin' undergroun'' where the Fleet brook joins the sewers,' announced Mrs O'Connor, for no reason at all that Aunt Irene could see. 'Sometimes when it rains like this they drahns, 'n' they come floatin' up the pan in people's barfrooms—all naked 'n' blind 'n' 'airless.'

'Phooey,' said Aunt Irene.

'S'true,' said Mrs O'Connor placidly. 'Me mum seen 'em.'

Aunt Irene gave up. 'A nice warming *tisane* is what I need,' she said, 'and some crispy, sugary *palmiers*.'

'You better 'ave a good meal,' advised Mrs O'Connor, ' 'cause Jimmy'll be 'ere soon wiv the boys, 'n' we don' know what time you'll get yer dinner.'

Aunt Irene had forgotten about Jimmy and the boys. Reminded, she regretted her earlier impulse. Her native indolence and goodwill had resumed their customary dominance over vengefulness and wrath. Her jaw dropped.

Mrs O'Connor, noting this, became bracing.

'Chirrup gel,' she said. ' 'S gotta be done. You'll 'ave no peace, else.'

'Peace!' remarked Aunt Irene eponymously.

'Jimmy'll jus' beat 'im abaht the 'ead 'n' neck wiv an ole railin',' Mrs O'Connor told her reassuringly. ' 'E won' 'urt 'im. No' a lot.'

Aunt Irene went pale and shuddered, like a blancmange. 'Oh don't,' she said.

Contempt sharpened Mrs O'Connor's tone. 'You gotta stand up for yerself,' she insisted. 'Don' let no one put nuffin' over on yer. You gotta bash 'em.'

Aunt Irene was presently averse to violence, haunted by the hanged man, and still deeply disturbed by the hanged woman. She felt strongly that no one should ever lay hands on anyone except in goodwill. It seemed strange to her that hands which must, in the nature of things, have implored and caressed could adjust the noose around their own or anyone else's neck. It seemed not to make any sense. It was dizzying. It bewildered her, as she'd been bewildered on learning of the martial consequence of cowardice. In the army *they shot cowards*. Homoeopathy, surely, carried to its wildest extreme. There was, thought Aunt Irene, a glaring thread of madness in human affairs which shed about it a short, confounding light towards which people were drawn like death-drugged gnats. She yearned for a clearer, wholesome light and, failing that, darkness.

160

It was growing dark. 'Valentine,' she called, as though for an emissary from a world less mad. There was about Valentine something of the ease and relief of a ghostless garden at dusk. She was unattended by the gibbering goblins of envy and frustrated desire which blurred and disfigured the outlines of most of Aunt Irene's friends. 'Valentine.'

'Aunt?' said Valentine appearing, soundless and shadowed in the doorway. She would call Berthe 'Mother', thought Aunt Irene, and felt for a moment that sense of endless loss that comes sometimes in dreams.

*   *   *

A faint whiff of decaying fruit hung about Reverend Mother's desk. She opened the drawer and surveyed the apple. It was definitely going off. Maculate, it had brown squashy areas, wrinkles and dents, and looked as though it might collapse in on itself. Reverend Mother prudently placed a sheet of blotting paper underneath it and sniffed once more, appraisingly, before she closed the drawer.

CHAPTER SIX

'Darling,' enquired Kyril as he entered the fragrantly lemon- and blood-scented kitchen where Aunt Irene was slicing liver. 'Why are there a lot of roughnecks creeping round the magnolia and hiding up lamp posts?'

Looking for Zachaeus, thought Aunt Irene. Zachaeus the publican, being short of stature, had climbed up a sycamore.

'They're Jimmy,' she said. 'One of them's Jimmy. He's brought his friends to intimidate the tax man.'

'They intimidated me, rather,' said Kyril. 'They're carrying bicycle chains and old chair legs.'

'I'd tell them to go away,' said Aunt Irene, 'only Mrs O'Connor would think me ungrateful.'

'Never,' advised Kyril, '*never* look a Trojan horse in the mouth—for fear of what you might see. What's for supper?'

'*Oeufs Florentine,*' said Aunt Irene.

'I always fancy the idea of *oeufs Holstein,*' said Kyril reflectively: 'one little egg perched riskily on another little egg.'

'Followed by liver, underdone, and tiny little new potatoes, and a salad of cucumber, cubed, not sliced, and a *tarte Auguste* gleaming with lightly fried lemons—and then I may shoot myself in the old Slav fashion.' Aunt Irene sat down, not in the rocking chair, which would have meant she'd completed her tasks, but at the kitchen table, which meant she hadn't. 'I have a feeling the reins have slipped from my grasp and the immediate future is out of my control.'

'It was never *in* your control,' said Kyril.

'My bit of it was,' protested Aunt Irene.

'Not at all,' said Kyril. 'An illusion.'

'I hope you're right,' said Aunt Irene. She was worrying herself quite out of her taste for dinner by permitting to nag away at her the fact that already there had been two hangings and things always went in threes. She thought, but didn't say aloud—what if Jimmy murders the tax man and gets caught and they hang him?

It would be uniquely embarrassing, would seriously interfere with her relationship with Victor and his mother, and it wouldn't do Jimmy a lot of good either. She was sufficiently depressed by thinking this when it occurred to her that she would, herself, be implicated, that she would be described as an accessory before the fact, that it might be suggested by Jimmy's lawyers (whom she already detested—she was beginning to detest Jimmy) that she had put out a contract on the tax man.

'It's a *nightmare*,' she said aloud. 'Do you think if I explained to them it was all a mistake . . . ?'

'No good,' said Kyril. 'They're enjoying themselves. Their blood is up. They've scented

163

the prey.'

'Pray is right,' said Aunt Irene distractedly. 'I think I will.'

She began by praying that Valentine was unaware of what was afoot, but she was interrupted by Major and Mrs Mason making a social call.

'Why are you doing this to me?' Aunt Irene silently apostrophised her Lord. 'Don't you like me any more?'

The Major and his wife said it was a terrible thing about Mr Sirocco. But they didn't seem to mind all that much. Mrs Mason's eyes gleamed dully, like sick fish.

The Major was startlingly, grimly sober, very clean, with a stark military demeanor and the clipped delivery of an actor who really had been a soldier and was now playing a soldier on the silver screen. When Mrs Mason tripped in her high heels on the edge of the drawing-room carpet, he revealed himself as the sort of man who, when a person accidentally drops a laden tray of food and drink or walks carelessly through a glass door, will point out at length that his action was foolish, misguided and regrettable. Aunt Irene thought if he was hers she'd kill him, and Mrs Mason didn't look as exalted as you might expect the wife of a miraculously reformed drunkard to look. She said, 'The Major doesn't want me to work any more, so if you don't mind I'm giving you a month's notice.' Her pleasure at thus inconveniencing Aunt Irene was noticeably marred by her resentment of the Major's officiousness.

The month's notice, thought Aunt Irene wrathfully, would be to give the Major time to seek gainful employment. She longed to mention that Claridges were looking for a doorman. He'd be perfect in the role, now he was so well-groomed and barking like Cerberus.

She had never, even in the darkest days of the war, been entirely without domestic help. Mrs O'Connor would, she knew, be delighted to give her a hand, but her sons wouldn't let her do menial work unless it was for them. Aunt Irene reminded herself that chars were like lovers. The sensible woman understood that they might not be forever and simply made the most of them while they lasted.

Mrs O'Connor came back from making tea for her sons at this point, and Aunt Irene went downstairs to halt the slow progress of dinner. She turned off the oven and put plates over things to keep the flies at bay. When she returned to the drawing-room the atmosphere there caused her to realise fully for the first time just how deeply everyone she knew disapproved of everyone else she knew. I'm a fool, thought Aunt Irene. It was stupid to house Kyril and little Mr Sirocco under the same roof. It was little short of cruel to throw together Mrs Mason and Mrs O'Connor.

She ceased these regretful reflections as she became aware that Mrs Mason was speaking.

' . . . and he says he won't have me in a house where there's a *nigger* . . .' she was saying, her weary face mottled like a foxglove's throat with horrid spite and triumph. She clearly hadn't forgotten that Valentine had forgiven her for her earlier display of prejudice. It must have been rankling and fermenting ever since. And as for the Major—if he by chance remembered the day the Devil sent his legions for him—he would detest Mrs O'Connor, who had physicked him, even more fervently than the divisions of class would dictate.

'Shouldn' fink 'e'd 'ave you anywhere,' remarked Mrs O'Connor by way of a shot across the bows, just to remind them she was there before hostilities really got under way. 'You silly ole mare.'

'That's right,' said the Major, agreeing with his wife's earlier statement and ignoring Mrs O'Connor for the time being. 'I know the native mentality, and I can tell you that miscegenation brings out the worst characteristics of each race. You'll always find your half-caste to be unhealthy and treacherous.'

'Nonsense,' said Aunt Irene. 'You're talking nonsense.'

She waited for them to get up and go. But they didn't. Astonishingly, they sat doggedly in their chairs, seemingly so moved by the topic

166

of race that nothing would shift them—not even the insulting presence of Mrs O'Connor.

'I know what I'm talking about,' announced the Major infuriatingly.

'Lady Diana agrees with us,' put in Mrs Mason. 'I met her in the butcher's.'

Briefly, Aunt Irene's butterfly brain tempted her to ask what Diana had been buying—she was still puzzled by the many-legged creature she had dined off recently—but she stuck to the point. 'Diana's a fool,' she said, flatly, and observed Mrs Mason's eyes flicker. She's going to tell that in Gath, she thought resignedly; she's going to publish it in the streets of Askelon. Goodbye Kyril's gallery. Let the daughters of the Philistines rejoice. 'You're a bitch,' she said, casting aside the last shredded rags of civilised intercourse and experiencing the odd relief of despair.

'Don't you talk to me like that,' said Mrs Mason. 'Lady Diana says you're *bohemian*.'

Well, so she was, thought Aunt Irene, just like Mrs O'Connor. Wanderers like tears on the face of the earth.

'*Ladies!*' said the Major.

'Aw, go spit in a bucket,' said Mrs O'Connor.

Kyril came in, followed by Cassandra, and looked amusedly at the angry faces before him. 'Good evening, my dears,' he remarked, and he shimmied a little as he came forward, in a manner calculated to madden the Major

167

to death. 'But how sweet you look,' he said to that poor soldier, 'so clean.' He turned to his aunt. 'There are fairies at the bottom of the garden,' he told her. 'They've come down from their lamp-posts and they're sniffing round doorways and dark corners in a very stealthy and ominous fashion.'

'Fairies?' said the Major meaningfully in a voice choked with disgust.

'Shut up, darling,' said Kyril without looking at him. 'If your mythical publican is there, Aunt, he'll soon be flushed out . . .'

And at that a howl rose from the street.

'Gone away,' said Kyril, and he made for the door.

'The horse Dulcefal,' said Aunt Irene to Mrs O'Connor, 'always knew precisely how any campaign would turn out. He belonged to King Hreggvid of Gardariki in Old Russia, and he could talk.' That would pay her back for the pigs in the lavatory pans, thought Aunt Irene, whose nerves had now brought her to the verge of the giggles.

Unmistakable sounds of the chase came in through the open door with horrid, joyful and entirely predictable cries of ' 'E went thattaway' and 'After 'im, lads'.

'They better not make that row,' said Mrs O'Connor nervously, 'they'll 'ave the coppers rahnd.' She followed Kyril.

'I don't know why she's suddenly so afraid of the police,' said Aunt Irene to Valentine in the hallway. 'She never used to be. It was always me worrying about the police.' She spoke in a whisper, since the Masons were still sitting, furiously still, in the drawing-room, the Major's trilby on his lap, Mrs Mason's dashing felt crammed over her brow.

'She doesn't want them to go to the Presbytery,' explained Valentine calmly. 'She keeps her stolen goods there.'

Aunt Irene gasped. She knew, of course, that the O'Connors had always had immense difficulty figuring out the nice distinction between *meum* and *tuum*, but she hadn't permitted herself to realise how far their activities went on the distaff side. She'd somehow assumed that only men were fully-fledged executive villains. 'Why the Presbytery?' she asked.

'Mrs O'Connor has the housekeeper in her power,' said Valentine. 'She says she'll tell the priest where all the butter and eggs came from in the war if she doesn't do as she's told.'

Aunt Irene reeled, physically. She put out a hand to steady herself against the hall table. 'How do you know?' she asked. She was quite certain Mrs O'Connor wouldn't have voluntarily disclosed this evidence of evil-doing to her saintly Valentine.

Valentine looked at her, unsmiling. 'I just know,' she said.

Aunt Irene shook her head as though cobwebs clung to it. 'Well, never mind that now,' she said. 'I'm going out to see what's going on. I'm going out,' she repeated loudly to her two guests.

They rose reluctantly and stumped out of Dancing Master House hard on her heels. She locked the door and said 'Goodbye' very firmly and sounding most unfriendly.

*   *   *

The magnolia put out a leaf to her as she passed, but she ignored it. The street was quiet and deserted.

'They went towards the river,' said Valentine, and it didn't occur to Aunt Irene to doubt her.

'I hope Kyril's not running,' she said; 'his lung won't stand it.' She herself broke into a fat person's trot and Valentine sped before her, silent as the passage of light.

Behind them, still intent on quarrelling and now also extremely curious, came the Masons.

CHAPTER SEVEN

'I never liked hunting,' confided Aunt Irene breathlessly to Valentine as they stood halted by the rush of traffic along the Embankment. 'Not wild boar, or moose or foxes or even mice—it's so *dangerous*.' She turned, and realised she was talking to thin air. Valentine must somehow have crossed the road to the river.

Aunt Irene took a breath and ran through the traffic, which seemed to rush at her, snarling and barking. 'Fry your face,' she directed a taxi driver who had stopped and was leaning out of his window, shaking his fist and telling her things about herself.

She stared to left and right and saw no one she knew. They could have chased him as far as the Houses of Parliament by now, she thought; and she cursed her age and weight, which normally she placidly accepted. 'Oh, damn everything,' she said, close to tears. She turned towards Albert Bridge and trotted past a large stone monument to a boiled egg in an egg cup with a snake wrapped round it, and then past the statue of St Thomas More, who sat on the other side of the road gazing, gilt-faced, eternally out over the river that had flowed through his life as now it flowed past his effigy. One of his martyred vertebrae was contained in a reliquary in Holy Redeemer. 'Pray for us,' panted Aunt Irene, to this leading member of an earlier Chelsea Set. She passed the statue of a coy girl, clad only in a thin layer of verdigris—so cold in winter, she thought irrelevantly. She was sure that in her ancestors' ice-bound land no one would set images of naked girls to face the frost.

'If you're looking for your nephew,' said a

breathless and unwelcome voice behind her, 'I've just seen him on the iron steps to the landing stage. He's with some very unsavoury-looking types.'

'Aaah,' cried Aunt Irene, terrified at the thought of Kyril adjacent to the river on those slippery steps.

And where was Valentine? What if the Frighteners had seized and broken her? What would Berthe say? Down river the birds would find her, thought Aunt Irene, and take her hair to nest in; and in all the trees the habitations of the birds would gleam and glitter, brighter than the leaves, fairer than the blossoms . . . I've gone mad, she said to herself. The awful circumstances of my life have finally driven me over the edge.

'There's something up,' said the Major darkly, and he went on to Albert Bridge to take reconnaissance down river.

*   *   *

Thus it was that the Major was the last person to see Valentine fly. A dark figure, treading air more lightly than any swimmer ever trod water, flew past his sober and astounded sight and dropped like a gull to the river, where a certain turbulence indicated that someone was drowning.

The Major turned, crossed the road by the lights, which fortunately were in his favour, went into the pub opposite and ordered a scotch. He was back on the bottle.

All the Frighteners, led by Jimmy, were dispersing as Aunt Irene dragged herself to the tiny landing stage. Like river rodents they slipped away to their secret haunts, leaving Mrs O'Connor to cope. Kyril was there too, noted Aunt Irene, relieved—and Cassandra. And Mrs Mason was leaning over the wall flapping like a wet kid glove. They were all staring at the greasily heaving surface of old Father Thames, and Mrs O'Connor was speaking. 'What the 'ell you doin' down there, Victor?' she was requesting in a low voice. 'You paddlin', or what?' She peered down the narrow flight of steps at her child, who was in turn peering intently at the water.

'I'm lookin' for 'im, are'n' I,' said Victor irascibly. ' 'F I see 'im, I'll grab 'im.'

' 'E c'd be down the Isle o' Grain,' grated Mrs O'Connor. ' 'E c'd be up the Prospec' o' Whitby.'

'I jus' seen 'im,' said Victor in a sort of whispered screech. 'Shuddup.' He crouched on the bottom step, holding on to the railing and reaching out.

A barge went by, lights gleaming fore and aft, and everyone pretended to be doing something to their hair or admiring the view, except for Mrs Mason who had elected to behave like the only concerned and responsible spectator at a crisis and was crying

173

'Police' and 'Help' and gesticulating. Aunt Irene kicked her.

The waters parted near Victor's outstretched hand, and a dark head and arm rose strongly. Valentine was bearing something towards the steps.

Victor seized her and drew her in. Together they hauled the sodden body of the drowned man to the top of the landing stage.

Mrs O'Connor bent her ear to his heart. 'Dead,' she said.

Valentine knelt over him and blew into his nostrils.

That's how they gentle horses, thought Aunt Irene, looking on in the peacefulness of shock.

'God rest 'is soul,' said Mrs O'Connor, as was her wont.

Aunt Irene looked more closely. 'Well, yes,' she said, 'certainly, but not yet. He isn't dead.'

'Yes 'e is,' said Mrs O'Connor, who had turned resignedly to the wall and was about to emerge on to the Embankment.

'No, he isn't,' said Aunt Irene. 'He's being sick.'

Mrs O'Connor turned back. It was undeniable that the dead were seldom sick.

She leaned over him, lifted his head and wiped his face with her hand.

'It's Stanley,' she said, 'from the Lambeth Palais. I reckernize 'im now wiv' 'is 'air all flat like that. 'Is wife got drahned overseas . . .'
She stopped speaking as the coincidental

174

implications of this were borne in on her.

'It's the tax man,' said Mrs Mason, forgetting her kicked and painful ankle. 'The debt-collector who came to see you.' She looked accusingly at Aunt Irene.

'Stanley,' said Valentine. She rose and went away, followed by Cassandra. They were soon out of sight.

Then Focus climbed out of the river, looking very little and thin, for the river water had driven all the air from his fur and it was streaming wet and sticking to his bones. In his mouth he carried a dead water-rat which caused him to hold his head very high—partly out of pride and partly to stop it sweeping the pavement—and he looked marvellously pleased with himself despite being so small and soaked.

Kyril stood with a lost and disappointed air, breathing in the ancient bitter smell of the river—one who lived for powerful excitement overwhelmed by anti-climax.

*   *   *

Miles away in Wales the drawer of Reverend Mother's desk smelled like a freshly tilled garden; of the dead who have finally returned, dust to dust; of earth. How odd, thought Reverend Mother, that this smell should fill the living with such hope.

*   *   *

As for me, the storyteller, I was in the pub by the river at the time, and drank beer and mead, but it all ran down my chin and none went down my throat.